Snows Run,
A Maryland
Mystery

By Linda A. Stewart

Author's Note

This is a work of fiction. Names, characters, places and incidents are either the product of the author's imagination or are used fictitiously. Any resemblance to actual persons, living or dead, events, business establishments, or locales is entirely coincidental.

Map Of Locations In Snow's Run

Cousin Farm

Snow's Rest

St. Mary's County

Porto Bello

Broomes Wharf

Snow's Run

St. Mary's River

Piney Point

Grasons Wharf

Chesapeake Bay

St. Mary's County

Potomac River

Virginia

Point Lookout Lighthouse

Linda A. Stewart

The Cawsin, Coode, Darberry, Price, and Snow Families							
Family Tree Coode, Cawsin, Price		Family Tree Darberry, Price		Family Tree Snow		Family Tree Cawsin	
Benjamin Thomas Coode b. 1837 d. 1902	Eleanor Mae Cawsin Coode (Wife) b. 1840 d. 1881	Carrie Frances Price Darberry b. 1847	Richard Enoch "Bud" Darberry (Husband) b. 1852 d. 1878	David Horatio Snow b. 1839 Missing 1863	William Thomas Snow III b. 1844	Jane Louisa Cawsin Snow (Wife Of Wm.) b.1846 d.1902	Ellen Frances Cawsin b. 1842 d. 1862
Benjamin Alexius Coode (Son) b. 1848 d. 1878	Mary Frances Price Coode (Wife) b. 1852 d. 1878	Richard Price Darberry (Son) b. 1873 d. 1903					
Thomas Alexius Coode (Grand-son) b. 1875	Ellen Mae Coode Abbott (Grand-daughter) b.1874 d. 1903						

Snows Run

Chapter 1: The Turning Leaf

That time of year thou may'st in me behold
When yellow leaves, or none, or few do hang
Upon those boughs...
William Shakespeare, (1564 – 1616)

Bright as ever, the sun hung on horizon's edge bathing river and field in blazing light. Bright as ever, water in Snow's Run below Snow's Rest flashed in setting sunlight. Water in St. Mary's River flowed on to the Potomac, on to the Chesapeake, on to the deep Atlantic. Walking uphill from field and barn, William Snow enjoyed the contentment resulting from a day's labor. He turned to behold the spectacle of water and sky as ever his ancestors viewed if for over two hundred years. Then he followed his shadow up the hill to his ancestral home, his summer retreat from Baltimore. As he passed the smokehouse, he noted the tree. Every year one leaf on one branch of the maple turned first to crimson and gold, heralding summer's decline.

Over the Rest's original English brick front, limbs of massive white oaks swayed to the waltz of an evening breeze. Jane's favorite Chopin, "Tristesse," floated through Snow's memory. A smile spread over his face as he recalled the nightly waltz. They swept across the torch lit portico, through double doors, and down the wide central hall. Paul Lundy, Jane's piano protégé, learned her personal arrangement of Tristesse by heart. Childless, Jane educated Paul, the gifted son of Snow's caretaker and cook. Each night brought a recital of Jane's favorites while Paul's mother prepared dinner. If Paul played Chopin's Waltz beginning in A minor, OP. 34, No. 2, Snow knew dinner would be late.

Milk sloshed out under a loose cover on the tin pail. As Snow walked up the hill, milk splashed onto his work overalls. With a frown, he examined the ground behind but saw nothing to trip him. He turned back up the hill towards Snow's Rest. A structure of many changes over two centuries. The original two-room, hall and parlor construction, sandwiched between gable end chimneys, provided a base for many renovations. Later revised to a central passage house with raised roof and dormers, the Rest now boasted a second floor. Snow had ordered a house kitchen added at the rear with an enclosed interior chimney to accommodate a wood burning stove.

Up the hill on the portico, a light appeared in gathering darkness. A kerosene lantern wick flickered and steadied to a glow as the glass chimney enclosed and protected the flame. Mrs. Carrie Darberry, William Snow's housekeeper, lit a lantern each evening to signal he was, once again, late for supper.

Then, she returned to the house kitchen to keep his meal warm.

Eight weeks after the death of her son, Carrie sailed into Snow's Run with a basket of food. She led Snow from the isolation of grief over the loss of his wife, Jane Cawsin Snow. Now, Carrie remained as William Snow's officious housekeeper and the only other resident at Snow's Rest. The milk reminded him of Carrie's admonishment to milk the cow dry twice each day. Otherwise, the beast would dry up after weaning her calf and leave them with no milk for winter. This only mattered if Snow wintered over at the Rest. When he sailed down in June, he had planned to return in September. Up the hill in lantern light, he squinted at shadows drifting across the porch. An image of Jane waiting on a wicker chaise, drifted through his memory. He longed for her gentle touch and blinked.

At the portico, he stared down at his mud-encrusted boots and recalled another of Carrie's admonishments. 'Sunday friends and family in the front. Barn boots in the back.' Two roses tied with a ribbon lay beside the light. Snow and Jane lost each of their two sons after birth. Jane's custom to place pairs of rosebuds in vases about the Rest comforted her grief for her lost sons. With the milk pail in his left hand, he turned down the wick to snuff the light. Then he walked the well-worn path around to the back yard. The roses remained abandoned to the night.

At the back of the Rest, the summer kitchen, separate from the house, sheltered in darkness. Carrie prepared meals there during the day. But, at the first approach of sunset, she adjourned to the inside house kitchen. Here she warmed late supper. She brewed a pot of tea on a wood stove in spite of summer heat. One evening after supper, Snow had invited her to join him on the front porch for a sherry while he sipped Melrose Rye. Eyes blinking, she glanced away, shrank inside crossed arms, and made her apology.

From the darkened yard, Snow studied Carrie as she moved about in kitchen lantern light. While setting a table for his supper, she glanced through the window into the dark yard. The pump handle creaked as he washed. She examined her reflection in the window and tucked loose strands into her tight bun. Snow finished, left his boots on the porch, and went in to supper, milk pail in hand.

Carrie Darberry greeted him. "You must be awful hungry this late. Tried to keep supper warm for you. It's a tad dry."

While smiling at her chastisement, he pumped two inches of well water into the deep sink, set the milk to chill there, and changed the subject. "I milked her dry tonight, but there's not much in the pail."

Carrie, her back to Snow while packing loose tea in an infuser, smiled. "Helps if you don't go waltzing with it." Snow winced.

Carrie continued dryly. "Your comrade in arms came by today looking for you. Wanted to give your heart a listen, I imagine. He brought that young Dr. Elliott for introductions. I sent them down to the barn, but they came right back up. Said you weren't there."

As the men in Carrie's family had fought for the Confederacy, she tended to refer to the Union with disdain. Dr. James Miles was drafted by the Union. As the local Medical Officer, Miles wrote draft exemptions for many St. Mary's County men. This placed him higher in her esteem than Snow, who volunteered.

"What did James have to say for himself?"

"You weren't at the barn. I made tea and we enjoyed a nice visit. Dr. Miles is thinking of retiring, or, at least, giving up house calls.   The new doctor, Bennett Augustus Elliott, is a Pottinger Creek West Virginia Elliott. The Elliotts who emigrated from St.   Mary's County around 1790. Some of his family remains on St. George's Island. Dr. Elliott lives at James' Great Mills house where he sees patients daily. James Miles only goes to Great Mills three days each week.   Now, the patients are only coming on those three days.   Of course, if the illness is serious..." She let the idea finish itself.

"I am sorry I missed them. I went over to Cawsin Farm for a while this afternoon. What did Dr. Elliott have to say for himself?"

Carrie took a kitchen towel off the plate in the warming oven. "Dr. Elliott has the youthful hope of changing old ways for the better. He sent for a trained nurse from the University Of Maryland School Of Nursing in Baltimore.   She will tend patients and make home nursing calls. She didn't arrive when he expected her. Hard to believe a trained nurse would come down here to work with a country doctor." She set the plate between utensils on the table.

Snow paused, his hand on the back of his chair, surprised at both Carrie's neighborliness and Dr. Elliott's ambition. "When did all this happen?"

"About the time I came to help you along. The first week in August." With the kettle set on the stove to boil, Carrie slumped into the kitchen rocker and fell to silence. Hands crossed and palms up on her lap, she sat still, her face weary with work.

Snow sat down to his supper, reflecting on the turning leaf, thinking about the front porch roses. A bake of layered chopped crab, cracker crumbs, and minced ham from Brome's Wharf store provided the main course. Beaten biscuits, slathered in fresh butter, accompanied butter beans and collard greens. The crabs came fresh from a trap tied to the pier in Snow's Run that morning. Butterbeans and collard greens grew in the back kitchen garden. Carrie churned butter daily by shaking skimmed cream in a mason jar and straining out the buttermilk with cheesecloth.

Several mouthfuls later, Snow looked up. "Thank you for supper. It's very good." He ate another mouthful. "I know you mean it as a comfort, but you don't need to leave the roses for me."

At first unheeded, his words hung in the lantern light. With a gradual turn, she gazed in his direction, her eyebrows lifted in surprise. Snow considered repeating himself but didn't.

Her eyes brightened, darkened, sharpened. "Where?"

Fork suspended, Snow feared he imagined the roses. "On the front porch table."

With one rock of the chair, Carrie lifted herself, reached for the kitchen table lantern and left Snow in darkness. She moved down the central hall to the foyer and out the front entrance. Weariness showed in her every step. Meeting her coming back in the door with roses in hand, he took the lantern. Snow felt relief he hadn't imagined the flowers. They went back to their places in silence. After settling into the rocker, she dropped the limp roses in the pail of kitchen waste.

More to herself than to Snow, she muttered, "Must have left them there by accident. Meant to leave flowers for Richard in the woods this afternoon."

Snow started at this revelation. Richard, Carrie's only child, died on the wooded path between Snow's Rest and Cawsin Farm. Images of Richard with his back bloodied from ax blows stabbed into Snow's memory. Now, he realized Carrie left flowers by the tree where Richard died. Reflecting that living at the Rest might not be the best situation for her, he returned to his cooling supper.

Rising from the rocker, Carrie tested the tepid kettle with her calloused palm. She tossed branches from the wood box into the stove's cast iron belly, onto smoldering ashes. The fire hesitated, blinking a few sparks as she poked the embers.

Perhaps the piney smell or the crackle snap of igniting pitch brought Snow to his feet. A shudder and a whoosh sent tongues of flame up curved lengths of stovepipe into the chimney. Snow slammed the bottom vent shut cutting air off from the flames. Sparks floated up into night as he stumbled into the back yard and looked up to the interior built chimney.

For centuries meals were prepared in a detached kitchen, now called the summer kitchen, and carried to the house. One summer, Snow faced a revolt from Jane. She refused to leave her modern Baltimore kitchen for a summer of the Rest's ancient detached kitchen. Snow agreed to the construction of an addition. Built as attachments to the central hall structure, the pantry hall and house kitchen had metal roofing. Sparks drifting in smoke from the chimney reached several feet above the house. Over Jane's opposition, wood roof shingles of the manor house were replaced with a metal roof. Snow's fear of fire overrode her objections to the deafening clang of rain on metal. Now, sparks fell down on that metal roof, and he counted each one as it winked to ash.

Snow's caretaker, John Benjamin Lundy, erected that chimney as the first step in constructing a house kitchen. He laid a base of ballast stones recovered from an old wreck sunk in St. Mary's river. Later, this former slave, born on Cawsin Farm, poured a foundation for hearth and chimney. Burning limestone rocks lay swollen in dying embers as John waited through the night for them to cool. In the morning, he poured water over the softened, smoldering stones that hissed, cracked, and turned to mush. Next, he added a mix of sand and gravel chipped from soft powdery rock outcrops along the Potomac River. When the concrete was ready, he poured it over the waiting ballast stones. Weeks later, with this firm foundation set, he laid a brick stove hearth and chimney with rear baffles allowed for heating the rear pantry and back bedroom. Lastly, he lined and faced the chimney with the same concrete mixture. John claimed fire would never burn through that lining to wood beams and horsehair plastered walls. Standing before the white monolith, he had announced this chimney would outlast the Rest itself. With arms held wide, he embraced the view of manor house, barns, wharf, and warehouse.

Decades would pass before Snow discovered these words inscribed on the back. 'This chimney built by John Benjamin Lundy, August 1887.'

Carrie's voice came to Snow from depths of shadow on the back screened porch. "We're out of firewood. I burn deadfall I gather from the woods."

"Perhaps, you should tell me." Snow's curt response resonated in amazement that a countrywoman would use dried pine branches, with cones and needles attached, in a wood burning stove.

She responded in kind. "Perhaps the next time, I will leave a note on your empty supper plate."

Snow returned to the cold, congealed remains of his meal, and Carrie withdrew to the back bedroom. In spite of three empty bedrooms upstairs, Carrie insisted on settling into the downstairs back bedroom just off the kitchen. She claimed the room was closer to her work. Snow gave up on his meal and scraped its remains into a kitchen waste bucket. After washing his dishes in the dishpan, he rinsed them in lye water, and left them on the drain board.

In a hope of making peace with Carrie, he trudged into the darkened back yard with the day's dishwater and the bucket of kitchen waste. In a wooded ravine far behind the Rest, he dumped the soiled water to avoid attracting animals to the house.

Snow gazed up at luminous constellations blooming in darkest night before the rise of the moon. He searched for Hercules who kneeled in prayer for strength and Draco, the dragon Hercules must slay to gain forgiveness. Driven by ravenous insects, Snow returned to the back, screened porch. Careful not to make a sound, he propped the dishpan upside down against a wall to dry.

Entering the kitchen, he eased the screen door shut so it would not slap closed on its spring. Carrie stood back to him at the dry sink in a pair of worn and faded slippers with a loose, partial braid down her back. The white of her shoulders and the curve of her hip shown through a thin summer night dress. Embarrassed for them both, Snow made a furtive retreat to the porch, scuffed his boots on the floorboards and cleared his throat. Carrie completed a slow turn towards the stove. With an unfocused gaze, she shuffled across the kitchen, bumped a chair, and stumble into the table. She picked up a long wooden match, and struck it against a black iron stove lid. The match broke. Snow tripped, sending the dishpan crashing to the porch floor board. As he bolted through the screen door, it slapped shut behind him. Carrie woke with a start and stared around in confusion.

She mumbled. "I see you're up in the night again."

"Sorry to startle you, Mrs. Darberry. I just dumped the dishwater."

"Well, thank you, but you can go up now." Carrie dismissed him as if he were a kitchen servant and retreated to the back bedroom.

Snow surveyed the kitchen and saw his empty dish back at the table next to the teapot in a pool of spilled water. Pocketing all the matches from the stove, he retrieved three boxes from the hall pantry. Lantern in hand, he made his way out to the summer kitchen, recovered the boxes there, and placed all matches in an empty milking pail.

Back inside, he poked the fire apart and doused remaining cinders with splashes of water from the kettle. After sweeping up loose tea, he toweled up the spilled water, eased down the lantern wick, and sat in fire light, waiting out the last embers.

Shadows, cast by fading light, brought to mind mysteries of misplaced and disturbed items. One morning he found the kitchen lantern in Jane's sitting room on Jane's piano. He declared nothing was ever to be put on Jane's piano. Carrie replied then he shouldn't put anything there. Another day, he found Jane's desk open with stationary scattered about. He said Jane's desk was not to be touched. He would buy stationary at Brome's Wharf store if Carrie needed some. Indignant, Carrie said she did not open the desk. She had her own stationary. If he wanted Jane's sitting room dusted and swept, he should take on the task himself. So, now he thought he knew answers to those mysteries. Carrie walked in her sleep.

Gentle as ever, a soft night breeze floated across the screened porch. Cool air whispered down the central hall to the house kitchen where Snow sat resisting the charms of sleep. He dozed in waning heat while memories of Chopin's Prelude Number 6 played slow and soft, easing him into night.

Floating at the edge of sleep, he drifted into a reminiscence of Jane. Fresh and lovely, she waited at an elegant table set with fine china and crystal. He spoke first. "Do you realize you're not real?" She remained silent. He challenged her. "Did we ever talk?" Her vacant eyes stared through him, and his body shook with a jolt as he realized the apparition had no mouth.

A faint hum whispered secrets through the cooling house. Waking to a sense of fading piano notes, he stared into vacant corners of the kitchen. He checked the dead fire, dumped the wood box in the back woods, turned the lantern wick down, he took the pail of matches up to bed.

In his room, he lit a candle to read by. Candle light flicked dusty shadows of insect netting against the far bedroom wall. One moth lifted in the updraft of candle flame, dropping back into brilliant danger. One mosquito flared out its spark of existence as Snow drift toward sleep. Myriads of insects trapped in folds of netting sang their notes of hope into the night. After closing his book, he rolled over and blew out the flame without raising the net or their hopes.

Behind Snow's Rest, woods that earlier swayed bright and green settled into night. A full moon lifted through the black tangle of wooden limbs. Above the sleeping earth, the brilliant orb waxed gold, heralding an imminent cycle of harvest. Moonlight bathed the Rest. Moonlight slipped through the grove of oaks and crossed the back screened porch into the house kitchen. Moonlight spread across river and field, illuminating the turning leaf.

Chapter 2: The Aftermath

When the summer fields are mown,
When the birds are fledged and flown,
And the dry leaves strew the path:...
Once again the fields we mow
And gather in the aftermath.
   Henry Wadsworth Longfellow,
   (1807 – 1882)

The setting moon drifted into an embrace of wooded limbs along the western shore of St. Mary's River. Cicadas sang their last nocturnal chorus. Tree frogs fell to silence. Owls winged to nest. Night relaxed its dark grip as fingers of sunrise spread gray light into an eastern sky. Pale streaks of pink caressed a scattering of feathered clouds dissipated by a predawn shower. Birds twittered among the trees and tuned before their first act. One rooster crowed. One luminous white pearl rose above the eastern edge of creation into a new day, the aftermath of all days before it.

While he listened to a wakening world, Snow dozed anticipating smells of breakfast and fresh ground coffee. Yesterday glided into his memory and reminded him to take the covered pail of matches back down to the kitchen. He rose, dressed, skipped his morning shave, and took the front hall stairs down to yesterday's aftermath.

As he walked down the dim central hall to the house kitchen, he encountered silence. Standing at the deep sink, he observed Carrie Darberry who sat still on a back porch rocker, still except for her hands. Rays of rising sun slanted through the porch catching in silver and gold strands of her twisted chignon secured by tortoiseshell pins. Rays of rising light flickered from a silver shuttle rhythmically tatting the lace in hand. From shadows of the house kitchen, he stepped into emerging daylight, pail of matches in hand. Knowing she heard floorboards creak his progress through the house but had not looked up, Snow pondered ways to improve his prospects for breakfast.

"Good morning, Mrs. Darberry" was met with a slight rise of chin, a slight pause of tatting shuttle. He retrieved the house kitchen match tin from the pail and carefully placed it before her on a back porch worktable, using both hands in a gesture of peace. His offer met a quick glance and a slight pause of the shuttle.

One gold strand of her chignon escaped coiling loosely over her shoulder, relaxing down her back. One gold hair pin secured the delicate chain attached to a pince-nez balanced precipitously between her eyes and the fine lace. Her country woman's big-boned hands, skilled strong hands, deftly tatted a delicate lace collar. Held nimbly in her left hand, the silver shuttle ending in a crochet hook worked in swift and smooth symmetry under and over, under and over, under and over a length of fine linen thread. Held lightly in her left hand, the thread grew a pattern of rings and chains. Calluses marked her fingers and thumbs where years and miles of thread had passed into her art. Double stitches, some with small open picots, looped along the collar's edge calmly creating a world apart from daily conflict. Stitch, darn, baste, tack, tat, all these made a women's world from a woman's hands, a world Snow had watched from a distance all his life. Carrie's small finger dropped the thread, created the knot, and the shuttle moved on. Another knot added itself to the delicate pine pattern collar growing in concentric lacey loops.

Heavy dew glittered with reflected sunlight as Snow crossed to the summer kitchen and began the morning's first fire. Finding ash in the firebox of the cast iron woodstove, he shoveled it into an ash bucket. Ash dust rose in gentle whirls and fell on his wet boots turning to a pasty pale reminder of all endings. Heavy dew anointed wild grasses and washed his boots clean as he searched for dry tinder along the edge between the yard and woods. After collecting yellowed grass, dried oak leaves, and small twigs, he searched for brittle branches in the shelter of larger trees. Under his boot, limbs of deadfall cracked and broke to kindling. Lifting branches against his heal, he judged their soundness for the fire by the crack, discarding greenwood that resisted his boot. Behind the abandoned caretaker's cabin, he found several pieces of split log, all that was left from the stack Piano Paul had split for his mother, Sarah. He took four splits to the summer kitchen and recalled Paul's massive arms; the ringing confidence of that brutal swing, ax against log, sledgehammer against iron splitting wedge. From the summer kitchen's opened doors, Snow glanced back across to Carrie's still figure tatting lace on the screened porch. Suppressed images of Richard's bloody death at the end of Paul's swing surfaced into Snow's morning. He dropped the splits. The moment passed, and Snow set the tinder and kindling in the stove's firebox. He opened the chimney damper and intake vent.

Passing back through the porch to the house kitchen, Snow hoped for a nod of acknowledgment but met none. He rummaged around in the pantry and was surprised to find a dusty tin coffee mill pushed far back on a top shelf. Beneath the lid of an earthenware jar used for coffee beans, Snow was delighted to find a new tin of Maxwell House coffee ground for immediate use in a percolator. Aroma escaping as he opened the can eased worry from last night off his shoulders. Pumping fresh water into the kitchen wet sink, he filled the percolator and spooned several measures of ground coffee into the metal basket, adding a dash of salt and a pinch of sugar. He secured the basket of grounds on the spindle that held it above the water and placed the glass topped lid on with a satisfied tap. Percolator in hand, he picked up the match tin on his way out to light the stove. He saw the slight curve of her smile.

While hoping Carrie had made her point and would cook breakfast, he attempted to light the tinder. Carelessly tossing in the first lit match, he met with defeat. He held the second match against dried oak leaves, moving it back and forth, watching them ignite. Damp tinder smoked, but still the fire rose among brittle oak leaves with a victorious snap. Kindling twisted to flame, and tinder collapsed to ash. Smoke wafted up the chimney as Snow added larger kindling and one piece of split log. He eased the intake vent. Light radiated from the fire's destroying force, filling rafters of the summer kitchen.

Leaning against a wood post that supported crossbeams, Snow studied footprints in the dusty earthen floor and waited for percolating hiss and pop, waited for rich coffee aroma to waft through the ancient summer kitchen shed, waited for liquid to bubble up darkly into the glass top. His waiting rewarded, he poured two tin cups of black coffee before placing the percolator on the attached side shelf to prevent bitterness from over perking. Hoping for amnesty, he walked his offering to the back porch along with a pot holder to protect Carrie's hands from the hot tin cup. She put down the lace collar and picked up the coffee. He met victory in her smile.

"Thank you, William. Good morning to you." After some blowing and sipping, she added, "I apologize for the pine knots last night. We're short on firewood. I had to gather deadfall along the path. It was getting dark, and I was in a hurry to get your tea brewed." Realizing she took the pine knots as his reason for confiscated the matches, Snow decided to leave her sleepwalking for a later discussion, or he might be back to baking his own breakfast.

"Carrie, I apologize for letting you run out of firewood. Thinking about it, I do believe you asked me to split some yesterday." She just nodded continuing to blow heat off the top of her cup. He remembered she always added milk. "Would you like me to get milk from the kitchen to cool your coffee?"

"Not this morning. It was too hot last night. Yesterday's milk has turned already. With the springhouse run dry and no ice, milk won't keep overnight. It might work for cream biscuits, but it would curdle in coffee." Snow's stomach growled with thoughts of Carrie's cream biscuits, an immeasurable improvement over his own hardtack breakfasts baked before her arrival.

Taking her comment as a good omen, he continued to sip. "I'll take a look at rebuilding the springhouse." Carrie raised an eyebrow that Snow took for skepticism. He took their empty cups out to the summer kitchen for more coffee and threw another piece of split log on the fire, anticipating those cream biscuits.

Returned to the house kitchen, he found her at the worktable surrounded by earthenware jars, tins of baking ingredients, flour sifter, bowl, salt cellar, two tin cups, fork, wood kitchen spoon, and a long charcoal iron baking tray. After blowing heat off the top of her second cup and taking a few sips, she began. Snow sat in the kitchen rocker trying not to finish his coffee too quickly. His empty stomach continued to growl.

Smiling, she scooped a second double handful of flour from deep in the barrel and slid it gently into a four cup flour sifter. She softly clapping flour dust from her hands, and without looking up, she commented, "I use two double handfuls, but you might want to make them scant." Snow looked at his hands, larger than Carrie's. In June, they were a lawyer's soft hands, but in August, they were a farmer's hands, hard with work of barn and field.

Opening the sugar jar to scrape the hardened block with a cooking spoon, Carrie pinched out enough to fill a well formed in the middle of her cupped hand and scattered it over the flour. Glancing up at Snow, she scattered another pinch into the flour before sprinkling in two pinches from the salt cellar.

Snow scrutinized her brisk and efficient manner in spite of sleepwalking the previous night. Thoughts of Carrie's pilgrimage yesterday along the wooded path to the bend by the large oak, the place her son Richard had died, made him speculate how often she had gone down that path. He thought about his previous day's visit to the house at Cawsin Farm, the house at the end of the same wooded path.

As an only surviving child, Snow's wife, Jane, had inherited that property. Over the years, she rented fields, pastures, and barns to cousins for tax money, but the house stood hollow. Trees crept a slow invasion, claiming fields, growing towards and into Cawsin farmhouse in determined eradication of the human footprint. Yet, the path remained and so did the footprints.

Snow watched Carrie's face, thinking she might have been there recently and left the new footprints in dust sifting through the old farmhouse. He prompted her with, "I was sorry to miss John Miles yesterday. I was over at Cawsin Farm, looking for anything that might be saved."

Snows Run

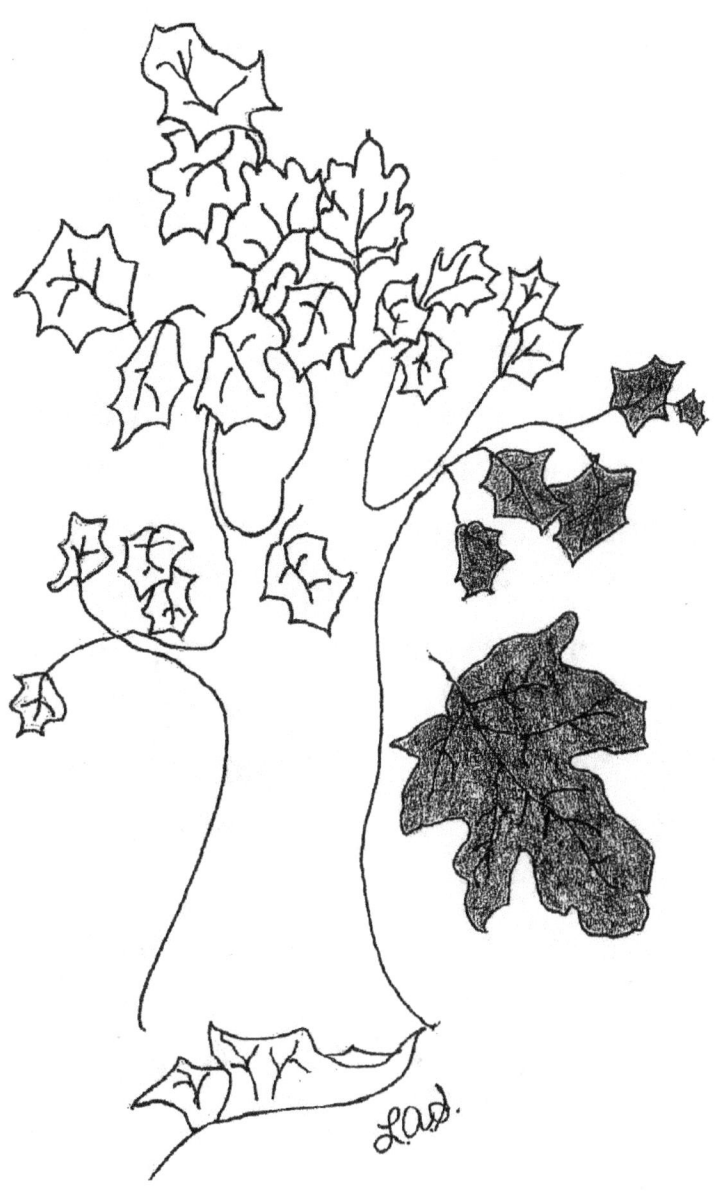

Instead, she countered with, "There's enough flour to get you through another week. Then you'll need another barrel. It's up to $4.45 a barrel for 140 pounds neat. In a stretch, one barrel would last you until February, but not the winter." He noted her emphasis on 'you'.

So, there it was, the unwanted guest, sitting in the kitchen waiting. Everywhere he turned the specter of change rose to greet him. It met him in the rising sun, in the coming harvest, in the turning leaf. Smiling, he mused at the humor of finding it at the bottom of a flour barrel.

"After this morning's chores, I'll take a look at the springhouse. See what can be done with it. We can buy another barrel next week from Broome's Wharf store."

Looking up from his coffee, he met another raised eyebrow as her hand extending the smaller cup towards him. "Pump a splash of water into this, just enough to cover a half inch off the bottom, and bring it to me." After a moment's resistance to her authoritative tone, he rose, took the cup from her hand and went to the sink.

Opening a tin of Patapsco Baking Powder, Carrie pinched a measure into the well of her cupped hand, about as much as the sugar, and sprinkled it into the sifter. White dust rose over the bowl as she turned the handle slow enough to sift, but keep her apron clean. As the last dry ingredients floated into the bowl, the pince-nez slid slightly. She tipped her head back and used the clean back of her wrist to tamp it back in place. Taking the water from him, she pinched another small amount of baking soda into the cup, about as much as the salt, and stirred it with a fork until it stopped purring. She handed him the larger cup.

"Skim cream from the top of last night's milk pail in the deep sink. Fill this cup until it reaches the first mark inside, about half way up." Sipping her coffee, she waited. When he returned with the soured cream, she added the water to it, made a well in the flour, poured in the liquid, and began to work solid into the liquid with a gentle regular motion.

Again, the pince-nez slid and would have fallen into the dough but he caught it in mid fall. The quickness of his hand surprised her, and she pulled back causing the attached chain to loosen a hairpin securing it. Gently, slowly, he reached into her hair removing the pin. Their eyes met. Her blush surprised him.

He broke the moment with, "I'll put this in the basket with your lace." She looked down into the bowl, went back to her spoon.

When he returned, she was scrapping the bottom, lifting dry ingredients into wet. "It's not beating hard that makes the biscuit nice, but an even lift of the hand

and elbow. If you beat hard it kills the dough."

Snow sipped his cooling Maxwell House and returned to Dr. Miles' visit of the previous day. "So, does this Dr. Elliott expect to pay a nurse out of his own pocket or is Dr. Miles taking on that expense as well?"

"That wasn't settled. When Dr. Elliott realizes he will be paid in chickens, eggs, and such, or maybe a ham for a difficult baby delivery, he may be just as happy that nurse didn't come. He has a problem with patients who don't follow his instructions and expects to send a private nurse out in a pony cart to check on them." They both smiled.

"This Maxwell House is excellent coffee. They served it on the *Anne Arundel* when I came down in June for the summer. How did you come by a whole can?" It took Snow a minute to realize that he had said 'for the summer'. Carrie glanced up from patting biscuit dough into a square, half-inch cake on a floured cutting board and nodded.

"Dr. Miles brought it yesterday. He is visiting farms on his house calls, introducing Dr. Elliott."

"I don't imagine he brought all his patients a can of Maxwell House."

"They were asking a favor." She began cutting the squares in two-inch pieces, poking them with a fork, and placing them in separate rows on the baking sheet. In an instructional tone, she added, "These biscuits take a quick oven. Place another split on the fire and open the vent some."

Coffee half raised to his mouth, Snow hesitated. She finished with, "Dr. Miles would like me to go on rounds with Dr. Elliott just until he knows his patients better, and they know him. Flora Miles and I will have to talk about living arrangements first."

He thought, "So, the lace collar is for Flora Miles, you will be assisting Dr. Elliott, and I will be baking my own biscuits.", but he said, "Just one split?" She nodded. Change, the inevitable, unwanted guest, watched as Snow sipped the last of his coffee and crossed to the summer kitchen, absorbing lessons from the aftermath.

Linda A. Stewart

Chapter 3: A Wandering Way

Alone in crowds to wander on,
And feel that all the charm is gone
Which voices dear and eyes beloved
Shed round us once, where'er we roved—
This, this the doom must be
Of all who've loved, and loved to see
The few bright things they thought would stay
For ever near them, die away.
        Thomas Moore (1779-1852)

Afternoon heat of August pressed down into fields, into barns, into Snow's Rest elevated above St. Mary's River in the shadow of towering white oaks. One red and white Jersey cow led her calf to shade along the woods and lay down to chew her cud. Standing head to tail under a majestic elm, the one horse and the one mule each took advantage of each other's tails to sweep away face flies.

Morning chores and wood splitting complete, Snow rubbed his farm overalls, smock, and straw hat with cedar and tansy oils to ward off insects. He rubbed a handful of wild mint over his face and neck before ambling through the woods to explore the springhouse. He was incredulous to discover it dry. The course of a spring flowing through this springhouse on this spot for two hundred and thirty years had wandered away. After circling the structure revealed no clue to the water's new course, he began a search through dappled sunlight along the woods. Snow worked downhill toward the river eventually reaching the mouth of Snow's Run.

The Run ambled a roving southerly course into St. Mary's River. The current twisted lazily in a torpid summer mood marking one boundary of Rest land. From its headwater in a heavily wooded hillside between Snow's Rest and Cawsin Farm, its late summer trickle, stained tannin by oak and pine, meandered along the streambed.

From the shade of old growth trees, the ribbon of water wandered into sunlight along cleared wood lots thinned by generations of his ancestors. It gathered waters from adjacent springs and flowed on passing cleared fields of tobacco and corn. Deeply scored by the flow of sporadic, seasonal deluge, the elevated edges of stream bank topped walls of crumbling clay and sand. They stood a man's head and shoulders over summer's dissipated trickle as the Run reached the River. Occasionally, these edges collapsed onto the stream, challenging its course. The water swelled behind and over all barriers, changing its path, but never its destination.

At the edge of water and land, wild grasses stood sentinel. As ever, rains of winter and summer gnawed stream bank from under their roots. As ever, foot and hoof trampled their leaf and stem. As ever, scattered seed continued to grow in triumph along the shifting edge. Snow tramped along in search of the wandering spring. Descending into the streambed, he uprooted grasses, scattered seed, and loosened a portion of stream bank. Layers of sand and clay slid into the Run's tea stained flow. Exposed from a sleep of three million years, ancient fossilized shells tumbled out of time under his boot. Once a vast ocean stretched above these empty shells of lost species, these mollusks never held live by any man. Once, endless waves rolled above them, racing on to heave relentless power against shorelines now rising as mountainsides in Allegany County.

Extracting a russet colored protuberance from the exposed stream wall, he discovered an entire Ecphora Quadricostata, a rare find. While brushing sand and clay from the elegant scrolling ribs and hollow cone-shaped umbilicus, he estimated its length. Held against his thumb, the ancient snail appeared greater than two inches, larger than any specimen in his Baltimore collection. Snow recalled the 1770 rendering in his father's copy of Martin Lister's Latin text, <u>Historiae Conchyliorum</u>, reputed to be the first published etching of an American fossil. Unfortunately, Snow had failed to rescue his father's copy from the fiery wrath of Edna Maud Snow's purge after her husband's death.

Avoiding the conflict between their father's science and their mother's God, William and David escaped to the woods and fields of Snow's Rest. Snow mused that while Lister's Latin text was lost to posterity, these fossilized snails still fell out of time into the Run and washed down St. Mary's River. He cupped the snail's tiny hollow umbilicus into his ear straining to hear the symphony of ancient oceans. Then he put the fossil into his overall bib pocket.

Extracting a gray scallop like fossil from the toppled slide of stream bank, Snow found it covered his outstretched hand. This specimen of Pecten Jeffersonius, first described by Lister in 1694, was used as bowls by early English settlers. It was later named in honor of President Thomas Jefferson, a naturalist in his own right. Snow caressed the ridges of its outer side, ridges like the waves of ancient oceans. He counted thirteen. Smiling, he remembered collecting these "unlucky ones" with his brother David. Deep in the woods, beneath layers of leaves and broken boughs of ancient oaks, lay the ruins of their childhood fort. They surrounded it with unstable stacks of "unlucky ones", an enemy they massacred daily.

Behind Snow, the *Bea Bee*, a skipjack with a black and yellow waterline glided under slack sail into the Run. Snow turned to see its lone occupant tie up to the dock, and disembarked with what looked like fish on a line. Snow waved from where he stood and watched Josiah Jenks trudge up the hill to Snow's Rest. Not looking in Snow's direction, Josiah failed to return the wave. Snow considered abandoning his quest for the wandering spring and walking up to the Rest. More than likely, Josiah was looking after Carrie's welfare, as he and his brother, Buddy, always had. If they wanted to talk to him, if Carrie thought the visit was important, someone would find him.

Continuing his exploration up the Run's right side into the partial shade of younger tree growth, Snow found another slide of stream bank. Here, winter's rush of snowmelt had washed away sand, tunneled under clay sediments, and left a cave-like outcrop. Under the shade of that outcrop, Snow's adjusted his eyes to dimmer light, blinking in anticipation.

Linda A. Stewart

Protruding down from the back of the cave, a dark grey-blue mass reached out from another century. Abandoned by the hand of man 260 years before the present, it waited. This sizeable piece of flint-like rhyolite, a lava form of granite, could only have come from the Catoctin Formation. Hewn from a Frederick County mountainside, it was traded along the shores of the Potomac River by tribes of the Piscataway Nation. This portion came to rest before a longhouse of the Yaocomico tribe on the shores of St. Mary's River. Long before Snow's ancestors lay claim to the Rest, this blue-gray rhyolite mass passed through skilled hands of an artisan to become the most valued possessions of his tribe. While warriors of his people eagerly waited for arrows and spears, this artisan knapped a pestle and abrader for the woman of his longhouse to grind corn. While the hunters of his people waited, he knapped a gorget, tied it with deer sinew, and placed it across his own throat for protection in battle. Then his hands and spirit, a spirit one with this stone, knapped out arrowheads and spearheads for feeding and protecting his Yaocomico tribe.

Snow advanced into the cave assessing the risk of dislodging the rhyolite. At his feet, a small dark point protruded from fallen soil. With bare hands, he gently unearthed a small triangular object with a contracted stem. Typical of Yaocomico arrowheads, its sharp, perfect edge showed lack of use. Snow placed it in the bib pocket of his farm overalls with the shells. Farther into the cave and directly under the rhyolite mass, something larger caught his interest. Crouching and finally crawling into the cave, he dug at what appeared to be the start of a substantial object, probably a spearhead. The point was perfect, but the shoulder and stem were rough and unfinished.

While pondering this mystery, Snow thought he heard his name. Thinking the sound just an echo of rising afternoon breeze against the back of the cave, he paused. Again, his name came drifting into the cave. Still holding the roughly hewn spearhead, he emerged from the cave to see Carrie Darberry standing downstream near the mouth of Snow's Run. Her country woman's holler, used to call family from fields to dinner, carried up the Run. Behind her, the *Bea Bee* slowly sailed out into St. Mary's River. Startled to see him emerge from under the earthen bank, Carrie placed both hands on her hips. Snow shifted uncomfortably like a school boy caught climbing too high in a tree.

She hollered, "I finished the wash. I will come back and call you. Bring more wood." Knowing this was his direction not to return while she was bathing in a tin tub on the back porch, he waved his understanding. With bathing as a Saturday routine, they both went their way to separate Sunday services clean and presentable.

Scowling at him, she scolded. "And if you don't stay out from under that overhang, it will collapse on you and the next service you attend at Trinity Episcopal may be your funeral." She reminded Snow of his mother standing there, scolding with hands on hips. He waved again and smiled. Carrie marched back up the hill. Snow meandered farther up the Run continuing his search for the wandering spring.

Ahead of him, blue and cream barn swallows dove in graceful twists hunting insects. They swiftly skimmed in and out of the Run's pooling lazy flow. Their twittering chatter turned to chirdeep alarms at his approach and back to chatter as he moved on. About thirty yards past the partially collapsed springhouse, the Run's course cut under the bank, intersecting the flow of the spring. Now it seeped into Snows Run well above the springhouse. In times of heavy rain, St. Mary's River sometimes flooded back up into the Run, carving an even greater wandering course. Walking up the cut, he examined the bank. Shredded remains of rotting irregular cut logs jutted out of the bank, some tipping over into the spring's flow as it rose over them and tumbled into the Run. A pile of Pecten Jeffesonias shells lay exposed in eroded sand and clay. Recognizing the location of his childhood fort, Snow spotted a dark object that protruded into the water's edge from under the collapse of an overhang. Something about the shape, or perhaps the texture, stirred him. He reached for it, closed his hand around it. Cooling air swept up the Run from under a lone gray cloud. Cold spring water oozed through the clay embankment on its way to fathomless oceans. At the moment of his recoil, he knew. Through all this day's wandering in dappled sunlight up this meandering stream, he was meant to cross her path, meant to cross her wandering way.

Chapter 4: Secrets

Nothing makes us so lonely as our secrets.
Paul Tournier, (1898 – 1986)

One fact was certain. A woman's black boot protruded from under collapsed clay embankment along Snow's Run, just short of Cawsin Farm. It could be, was most likely, Hattie Maud Wells' boot. Hattie who was missing and assumed drowned, whom all assumed had murdered at least once. At that moment his mind flashed back to June, to Darberry Farm kitchen, to watching Hattie raise his 1902 Sport Model Colt revolver, to watching her point it at him. Trapped in that past moment, he stepped backward towards the remembered open farmhouse door, splashing into the Run instead. Wet to the knees, Snow came back to the present. Wondering if this boot, buried in mud, had washed downstream or flooded up from the river he took a deep breath and stepped closer. After reexamining it, Snow used the *Pecten jeffersonius* shell from his overall bib pocket to excavate through the adhesive sucking wall of clay. He stopped where a leg protruded from within a woman's boot. As he stepped away, he stumbled against a fallen red oak and sat among its bare, topmost branches now sprawling into the Run. He lost track of time until the hoot of an owl hunting in late afternoon disturbed his thoughts.

Remembering Benjamin Franklin's admonition that three could keep a secret if two were dead, Snow resolved not to say anything about the body in the Run to Carrie Darberry. Until Sheriff Freeman knew, he would not tell anyone. Snow hoisted himself up the embankment in view of Cawsin Farm. Dilapidated crumbling structures, an unkempt graveyard, and fallow fields were relics of Jane's family farm. Oppressive heat in late afternoon added to the melancholy settling over him. After several deep breaths, he turned his back to death and ruin before heading down the path between Cawsin farm and the Rest.

Cooler woodland air pushed through overgrown brambles along the path drying his wet and clinging muddied clothes. Afternoon drafts of piney fragrance played through the canopy of oaks, pines, and tulip poplars, carrying memories of clandestine meetings between Cawsin girls and Snow boys. Childhood memories of hidden letters, a secret rendezvous, a first kiss, all lightened his heart as he moved toward the bend in the forest footpath. A vision of his beloved Jane settled gently into his thoughts.

Head down, watching his step, he tramped along brushing against intruding overgrowth. Scent of roses wafted through the trees as he looked up to a vision in a summer sun hat floating in flowered chintz and almost walked into Carrie Darberry. She stood still as a deer watching him come, a bouquet of late summer roses in her hand.

"I thought you might be here," he said.

"Did you?" He caught her tone of skepticism, as she surveyed his mud covered clothes and boots. "Have you been up to Cawsin Farm again?"

She turned off the trail toward the ancient oak at the bend in the woods, the oak where her son, Richard, had died. She propped the roses up against a curve at the base of its trunk. After succumbing to Hattie Well's charms, Richard had made a discovery that drove him to attempt Hattie's strangulation. Paul Lundy, Jane's protégé and master of both Chopin's classics and Joplin's ragtime, had put an end to that attempt with an ax under this tree.

Snow just nodded yes and turned to stand beside her with his head bowed in prayer. Carrie made a sign of the cross, and they stood together several moments before starting back to the Rest in silence.

Tin bathtub, soap, scrub brush, two Turkish towels, and clean farm clothes awaited him in the summer kitchen. Hot water simmered on the stove, ready for pouring into cold bath water. Carrie announced she would tat lace on the front porch after collecting eggs at the barn.

Refraining from mentioning that he collected eggs every morning, Snow nodded, kept his silence, kept his secret like a stone in darkness. Stone can be a pebble, rock, or boulder, can grow to weigh a mountain over time. Stone can be a pit, kernel or seed, can sprout, leaf, and bloom to undeniable deception.

Freshly bathed, Snow dressed in clean linens, farm shirt and overalls. He placed artifacts from the Run into the overall's bib. Then he dumped the bathwater in a wooded trench behind the summer kitchen and tipped the tub against a wall.

He poured himself three fingers of Melrose on his way through the house. From his carved oak and cedar lined cigar box, he chose one that Thomas Alexius Coode, distant cousin of Jane Cawsin Snow, had given him the week before.

Orphaned when the steamship Express sank off Point Lookout in 1878, Thomas and his sister, Ellen Mae, were raised by their grandmother. After the grandmother's death, Carrie had gone to care for them at Jane Cawsin Snow's request. Now, Thomas was the new first mate of the Weem's Line steamship, *Northumberland*. On last week's visit, Thomas had brought a bolt of navy blue gabardine cloth for Carrie and twenty of Fader's IRABA cigars, Snow's favorites. They were manufactured on Water Street in Baltimore by Ira Fader, a Johns Hopkins University-educated chemist and son of the German-born founder of Faders Cigars, Abraham Fader. A political supporter and occasional guest in Snow's Baltimore library, Ira always brought a gift box of these cigars advertised as an 'eight cent cigar-something to look forward to.' In addition to the IRABAs, Thomas brought a solid silver curved box containing 10 Van Bibber Little Cigars manufactured by H. Ellis & Company on the corner of Lombard and Charles. He explained that smaller cigars were preferable when a man was working with travelers or cargo and didn't have time to enjoy a real smoke.

After dinner when Carrie excused herself and retreated to her room, the two men adjourned to the screened portion of the front porch. They sipped Melrose Rye, drew on their cigars, and took turns blowing rings into the stillness of the evening.

As the whiskey took hold, they recited the first lines of Thomas Hood's <u>The Cigar</u>,

> Some sigh for this and that,
> My wishes don't go far;
> The world may wag at will,
> So I have my cigar.

They moved on to lines from Kipling's poem, <u>The Betrothed</u>,

> Which is the better portion
> Bondage bought with a ring,
> Or a harem of dusky beauties,
> Fifty tied in a string?

Eventually, Thomas confirmed Snow's suspicions by turning the conversation to Hattie Maud Wells. When Hattie was a child, Thomas was her protector. He protected her to the point of violence that nearly landed him in prison and did send him into the cavalry where injury left him with a slight limp. When Hattie blossomed into womanhood, Thomas had loved her, asked for her hand in marriage. Escorted on Thomas' arm the day of Ellen Mae Coode Abbott's funeral, Hattie had attended as the fiancée of Thomas Alexius Coode, brother of the deceased. Sometime late on that day, after the reading of Ellen's will, the couple had parted in disagreement, the engagement broken. Rejected by Thomas, Hattie had fled first into the arms of Richard Darberry. Later, rejected by Richard, she had turned to Paul Lundy, setting off a chain of events leading to all three deaths, or possibly only two and Hattie's disappearance.

As Thomas sat beside him that night, Snow recognized grief in Thomas's face, recognized regret. Recalling his own grief for Jane, Snow wondered if Thomas saw visions of Hattie in the corner of his eye or across a crowded room. He wondered if Thomas heard Hattie's footsteps on quiet nights. Thomas asked if there was any sure sign of Hattie's fate, but Snow had nothing to offer. Snow asked Thomas about the broken engagement. Thomas only stared through the soft gray veil of cigar smoke into the hush of twilight when air of field and river meet in peace along the shore. They inspected rings of cigar smoke melting into deepening shadows. Dim torchlight revealed Thomas' premature gray at the temples and shadowed eyes. Snow suspected Thomas felt more than grief, suspected he felt guilt and unending uncertainty. For a moment, Snow had thought to show Thomas the photograph of older brother David's Texas family, a photograph that probably included Hattie's mother. Contemplating the possible consequences, he reconsidered. Now, staring down into his cigar box, Snow fingered the firm brown IRABA and slid it across his face to inhale the fermented spicy scent. He wondered what he would say to Thomas when next they met. Snow returned the cigar to the protective cedar lining and closed the box lid back over it.

Tonight, sitting beside Carrie on the front porch, Snow let the peppery taste of whiskey ease the tensions knotting muscles of his neck and back. As he sipped, Carrie tatted the lace collar, the last loop, and then the last knot. Sighing with the relief of a task finished, she smoothed and folded layers of blue tissue paper over it with her callused bony hands.

Snow sipped his Melrose. "That lace is beautiful, a work of art. Will you wear that to mass at St. Ignatius tomorrow?"

At first, Carrie stared at him in silence until he thought she hadn't heard him. Then she snapped, "This is a gift for Flora Miles.", and left for the kitchen.

Each Sunday, Snow drove his carriage to Dr. Miles' Bluestone Farm, leaving Carrie there before driving himself to Trinity Episcopal. The Miles took Carrie to Catholic mass at St. Ignatius down on St. Indigoes Manor, and they would all picnic together after Mass. One of Flora's grandsons would drive Carrie back to Snow's Rest before evening. But, that would be tomorrow.

Late afternoon rumblings announced thunderheads rising over trees across the River. Snow sipped his whiskey and listened for sounds of Carrie preparing their country supper, a homegrown meal with very little store bought. Curiosity and appetite led Snow to amble back down the central hall, leaving the front double doors open to funnel a hoped for evening breeze through the Rest.

In past years, he rarely trespassed into Jane's kitchen, and he still hesitated at the door, feeling like an interloper. The stove was cold; the fire unlit. He cleaned ashes from the firebox and prepared a fire with tinder, kindling, and one split. From the summer kitchen wood box, he retrieved more splits and moved the tin of house kitchen matches from the back porch to the stove mantle. Then he sat, sipping and waiting for directions which were not long in coming.

Dumping fresh shelled lima beans and water into the base of a two quart double boiler, Carrie added salt, pepper, and a pinch of sugar. "You may start the fire now."

Snow opened the chimney vent, lit the tinder, poked at igniting kindling, and slid stove vents open. As a draft rose under the fledgling fire, Snow relaxed and considered his part in the preparations complete.

From a bowl of water containing nine eggs, Carrie lifted out two rotten ones that floated above the others. She deftly placed these in a bucket of kitchen waste so as not to break them and fill the kitchen with their rotting smell. "It's important to get every egg every day from the laying hens. Did you find that wandering spring of yours?"

Snow sipped and carefully measured out a grain of truth. "It looks like the Run cut across that spring farther up towards Cawsin Farm. It doesn't flow down to the springhouse anymore."

Carrie let the silence spread through the kitchen like runny batter on a griddle, before ordering, "I need the lantern lit."

Irked by her imperious tone, Snow retrieved the match tin, placed it next to the lantern, sipped, sat, and stood his ground waiting for her to light it herself. Silence settled between them.

From the back pantry, Carrie retrieved a cleaned medium sized rockfish with its tail secured to its head and soaking in salted vinegar. She pumped cold water over the fish in the deep sink and placed it to steam covered in the double boiler top above the lima beans. Vinegar tang filled the kitchen, as juices from the fish dripped into the beans sparking Snow's appetite.

After adding more water, she responded to his questioning look with, "The Jenks came by today when you were wandering around up the Run. Brought us this nice rockfish. They are wondering how we are getting on. If you want a fresh omelet, you will light that lantern."

An eatable omelet being preferred, he lit the lamp and observed her candle the eggs with its glow. One of the seven eggs darkened when held up to the light, so she placed it in the waste bucket with the other rotten eggs for the pig. She grated crumbs of dry rye bread into a small bowl, pinched salt and sugar into them and ground something over them before adding milk. Snow thought he smelled nutmeg.

While taking care not to reveal he had seen Josiah alone, Snow asked, "So, what did Josiah and Buddy want this time?" For that remark, he got a sharp look.

"Sorry, I didn't mean it quite that way."

"Do you always talk like a lawyer?"

Snow considered she would make a good prosecutor but deferred from that comment. She was cooking his dinner.

Setting aside the softening crumbs, Carrie cracked four good eggs into a basin. Then, she used a piece of egg shell to remove the white treadles that connect egg yolks to shell. "It was just Josiah. Buddy took work at Broome's Wharf delivering ice. Josiah said he looked up the Run but didn't see you. Must have been when you were messing about under that overhang. Don't know what he meant to ask you. He asked me what I planned to do about Dr. Elliott."

Carrie checked the water level in the double boiler. Then she placed it on an attached cast iron side shelf to prevent the lima beans from burning or the rockfish from steaming dry. She began lightly whisking the eggs.

Snow received a brief smile when he took down plates, forks, and cups for water and tea. He pumped a pitcher of cold water and filled the kettle to demonstrate he wasn't completely helpless. After setting plates and forks at a table on the cool, screened back porch, he lit a torch of cedar oil mixed with tansy and sassafras root to discourage mosquitos. He returned for napkins and took down the tea ball and pot.

Carrie was quick with, "I'll take care of tea. Josiah brought you something besides a fish. It's in a mason jar on top of the icebox in the back pantry." Snow stood, holding the teapot and ball suspended in surprise, a frown wrinkled across his forehead.

Carrie stopped beating the eggs. "As there is an icebox under all those old quilts in the pantry corner, there is no need to rebuild the springhouse. I gather the icebox was hidden from your view? You do know a refrigeratory icebox was patented by Thomas Moore of Silver Spring one-hundred years ago? You do realize we have ice delivered all the way down here in St. Mary's County?"

Snow considered whether her comments were statements of fact, questions, or reprimands. While retrieving the mason jar of Jenks Best corn whiskey, he looked under a pile of quilts and found an icebox. It occurred to him Buddy was delivering more than ice on his rounds.

Returning to the kitchen, he explained, "When we lived in the Hamilton Street house, Jane bought a larger icebox. When it arrived, I hired a carpenter to enlarge the kitchen pantry as I didn't want the thing taking up space in the back parlor. It never occurred to me she had the smaller one brought down to the Rest."

Snow sat, sipped, and watched Carrie plop a dollop of newly churned butter in a large black skillet heating on the stove. She added the soaked crumbs into the eggs and continued beating vigorously while watching the butter melt, bubble, and start to brown.

While pouring the egg mixture into the skillet, Carrie casually asked, "So what else did you find up the Run?"

For the flash of a second, Snow thought she knew. While lifting a sip of Jenks Best to his lips and counting a few heart beats, he decided she didn't. He let a bit of truth sprout and leaf out to cover the spreading secret. He took the fossils from his overall bib pocket and placed them on the kitchen table for her inspection.

"When we settle down to supper, you might find this interesting. It was under that overhang."

Without looking up, she lift sides of the breaded omelet, letting liquid egg run over into bubbling butter. A mouthwatering nutty, buttery, sweetness wafted from the stove.

Pushing her hands into what looked like two oversized leather mittens, Carrie lifted the double boiler and placed it in the deep sink. Snow brought her the plates. She divided the fish, spooned up lima beans, drained them against the side of the boiler, and spread them over portions of fish. She dropped the last two eggs, still in their shells into the steaming water to harden. She stared straight at him and asked, "You were gone quite a while. Was that all you found?"

After turning the omelet, she folded, divided, and lifted halves onto plates before garnishing them with sliced peaches and a spoon of strawberry preserves.

To escape the kitchen heat, they sat at the back porch table, where they usually ate evenings. Not once since her arrival, had she served dinner on china in the dining room. They said a silent grace. She crossed herself. He didn't. Once again, he offered her a glass of sherry, and she declined. She waited for her answer. She had not lifted her fork: he could not start his meal.

"I found these few intact fossils for my collection in Baltimore. My father's collection is there, and I add select specimens when I find them. There's nothing you haven't seen before." With the fossils on the table, he kept the spearhead in hidden reserve. She picked up her fork. They ate in concentrated silence, consuming the salty, vinegary flaky white fish balanced with the sweet and sour of the lima beans before starting on the nutty bread omelet.

Carrie broke the silence. "Josiah is asking if anyone saw a stranger, a woman with a carpetbag and a smaller black bag, walking towards St. Mary's Seminary from Broome's Wharf. This would be during the last week in July. He's asking for Buddy who saw the woman and is concerned about her for some reason."

Swallowing a partially chewed mouthful, Snow chocked and washed it down with water. He shook his head and shrugging his shoulders to delay comment.

Finally, he asked. "Dr. Elliott's nurse?"

"Maybe. This was all before I came. Buddy took his time asking about her. Seems he didn't think much about seeing her until this last week when he heard that Elliott sent for a nurse and couldn't find her. It got Buddy thinking you might have seen her."

New possibilities bloomed and withered, choked off by secrets he had planted. A jungle of half-truth and omission left him to consider Carrie's reaction when the truth was finally known. One bit of evening breeze tumbled spent rose petals from Jane's garden through the back yard.

Over tea when supper was done, Snow placed the spearhead and arrowhead on the table next to the fossils. Carrie picked up the spearhead running her hands over it.

"Strange it isn't finished. Something happened. He died."

"You got that from running your hands over it?" Skepticism tainted Snow's response.

"No. I got that from logic. The stone is good, no cracks, perfect but not finished. What would keep the knapper from completing it? Only death would keep him from his purpose."

"I see. So, what do you think happened to him?"

"The usual; war, pestilence, or old age. Things that get us all in the end. Whatever it was will always remain his secret." Snow let her statement end the conversation. Tree tops whipped as the chill of an evening squall passed over the Rest, streaming rain through field and wood, rain that flowed into the Run, washing over all its secrets.

Linda A. Stewart

Chapter 5: Revelations

Not "Revelation" –'tis-that waits,
But our Unfurnished eyes...
 Emily Dickinson (1830 – 1886)

Walking through dark water to a drum's cadence, Snow searched for his .44 caliber Henry repeater rifle but found a wooden match in its place. He struck it, and the flame lit dimly familiar faces on fog-shrouded shapes sitting by firelight. Stumbling towards the campfire, he reached it and squatted among soldiers. One soldier stirred green coffee beans that roasted in his mess kit kettle before mixing in crushed chestnuts, rye grains, and raw sugar. An old man's hand reached from inside the union uniform sleeve of Snow's youth and poured more water into the kettle from his canteen. John Benjamin Lundy, Snow's slave child companion, floated reclining below the soldiers, a wooden topped coffee pot in hand, and poured steaming brew into tin cups. Brother David in frayed Confederate rags materialized from the fog to trade tobacco and whiskey for coffee or pork and eagerly drank the dark brew. Above the mist, their mother, Anna Maud Snow, floated and smiled dotingly on David, her eldest son. Across the rising smoke, a woman clad in a blue linen suit stood with her back to Snow. She turned to face him before slipping behind a pink chintz curtain. A blast shattered the night. He felt the kick of his 1860 Henry rifle shake the bed waking him from the gods and demons of his dream. The aroma of Maxwell House coffee drifted through the Rest.

Snow woke from a restless sleep to the frail light of impending dawn. His thoughts turned to coffee and breakfast. Ignoring his Sunday dress suit, brushed and laid out the night before, he put on the coming week's clean work overalls. He shuffled his way down to the house kitchen. A coffee pot, keeping warm under towels, waited on the kitchen table. He filled a tin cup. Carrie wasn't in sight, but he expected she was down the path refreshing Richard's flowers. With that thought, he strolled towards the rose garden taking a grass scythe to trim Jane's grave. In the pleasure of dawn's early chill, insects had yet to stir. A robin trilled "cheerup" from the garden's edge, and a rufus-sided towhee answered "drink-your-teeaaa" from the forest canopy. He trimmed Jane's grave and around David's memorial.

When he was part way through the parental graves of William Thomas Snow II and Anna Maud Snow, Carrie walked grim-faced from the wooded path to Cawsin Farm. She marched across the back yard in her faded farm dress, drenched and spattered in mud, with a shovel in her hand. The shovel clattered down on the steps as she entered the back porch and let the screen door slap shut behind her. With coffee pot and a tin cup in hand, she returned to search the yard for him. After pouring for them both, she picked two roses for Jane's grave and handed them to Snow. Not a word passed between them, but he knew she knew.

Peering at Snow from under her frayed straw sunhat, she exhaled a deep, tension relieving sigh. Gently she said, "William, you can't keep this a secret."

"Carrie, it is my intention that Sheriff Freeman knows first. I assumed it would upset you. So, I decided to wait until he arrived. Can I ask you not to say anything to James Miles today, to wait for Freeman?" They sipped coffee. He hoped for her assurance.

Instead, he got, "Sheriff Freeman will ask Dr. Miles to be here when her body is removed from the embankment. Also, we should consider where to bury her. That is if she is Hattie Maud Wells."

"True. I hadn't thought of a funeral. How did you know?"

"Last night, when I told you that Buddy Jenks might have seen Dr. Elliott's nurse, you wanted to say something, but you choked it down. At that point, I suppose you couldn't tell me. Secrets grow a tangle."

They sipped coffee, giving him time to consider. "Yes. Well, another thing I didn't tell you is the reason I hid the matches yesterday. The night before, you were sleepwalking in the house kitchen, and tried to light the stove." He kept it simple, watched her surprise turn to acceptance and dismay.

Carrie followed several moments of silence with an officious, "I'll start breakfast while you do your barn chores." They went their separate ways, hurried by the need to leave for two separate church services.

Taking the kitchen waste bucket, Snow trotted downhill to the barn and tossed the contents with a few dried corn ears to the pig. A refrain of happy grunts greeted him. He put the mule and the weaned calf out to pasture, but they only paced to a fro outside the barnyard gate. After throwing the old carriage horse Jake and the jersey cow forkfuls of spring hay sweet with clover and timothy, Snow sat on the milking stool. With his forehead pressed to the cow's contented side, he milked her dry. Meandering out to the water trough after he turned her out, the Jersey gazed expectantly at him, her huge pink tongue wetting her nose. Snow primed and worked the pump until the water trough was full and ran over into the yard for mud to cool the pig. Carrying two buckets of water to Jake who stomped impatiently in his stall, Snow smiled at

Floppy. The mule looked quizzically at Snow over the pasture fence, waiting for his old friend Jake. Snow currycombed, brushed, and harnessed Jake while the mule drooped his head in disappointment and slowly strolled out to graze alone. After rubbing Jake down with tansy and wild mint oil, Snow walked the reluctant, hoof dragging beast up to the Rest. With time growing short, Snow left egg collecting for later. Using Jake's halter lead, he tied him in the carriage shed and drew him another bucket of water.

Breakfast was simple; refried biscuits, preserves, hard boiled eggs dipped in salt and pepper, sliced peeled peaches, and coffee. After a quick wash and shave, Snow donned his Sunday best, hitched Jake between the shafts of the Courtland Surrey, and they were off to Bluestone Farm. In her white-gloved hands, Carrie held a small basket with the blue tissue wrapped lace collar tucked into the bottom.

Turning onto Mattapany Road, Snow ended the silence with, "I had a dream this morning about making coffee in the army. Waking up to that Maxwell House is a considerable improvement."

Carrie smiled. "Are you certain what you drank in the army was actually coffee?"

He shrugged. "If we were lucky, we had a few green coffee beans to roast with whatever we could forage." He paused. "So, what are you going to tell Dr. Miles?" She didn't answer.

A letter to Sheriff Freeman, scratched out by candlelight the night before, rested in Snow's left inside pocket. Originally, he had planned to drop this one and a second letter to his Baltimore law office in the mailbag at St. Mary's City Post Office. Postmistress Susan Bennett Abell left the bag on the porch for the convenience Sunday church goers. Instead, he decided to find someone willing to sail Freeman's letter to Leonardtown this afternoon and deliver it to the Sheriff in person. A wax seal placed over the envelope flap this morning would hopefully secure the secret inside.

With services at Trinity Episcopal complete, Snow found two teenage grandsons of Cousin Enoch Snow willing to deliver the letter for a dollar. He offered them another dollar if they returned by tonight with a reply. The young fellows pushed off towards Leonardtown in a sloop rigged crabber about 24 foot in waterline. They took a picnic basket and two friends, all of them excited to be on an adventure.

Snow posted the Baltimore letter and retrieved the mail from the post office, left open for convenience on Sunday, before heading towards the Rest. Needing no direction home, Jake picked up a brisk trot, and Snow fell to thinking over what Carrie said about Dr. Miles and a burial.

At the turn off to Snow's Rest Road, James Miles waited with Carrie in his one horse high-wheeled doctor's carriage. Snow was not surprised. Another younger man waiting on horseback was introduced as Dr. Bennet Augustine Elliott. The introduction included his descent from the Elliotts who emigrated from St. Mary's County to Pottinger Creek in Nelson County, Kentucky sometime around 1800. Snow leaned over his carriage wheel to shake Elliott's hand and welcome him home to St. Mary's. Elliott brightened, and both doctors seemed cheerful which confused Snow until he caught Carrie's cautionary head shake.

James Miles next comment explained his presence. "Well, William, my Flora has sent me to deliver a sumptuous picnic and introduce you to Bennet Elliott." Snow was amazed Carrie managed to get Drs. Miles and Elliott here without revealing there was a body in the Run. He understood when

Miles tapped the doctor's bag under his seat. "Thought we might have a look and a listen while we were here."

Smiling, Snow acquiesced with "Well, I hope you have that trap baited with Flora's fried chicken." They all proceeded at a trot down Snow's Rest Road anticipating the big Sunday picnic.

After unpacking, tending to the horses, and washing at the pump, they sat down at the back porch table spread with table cloth, plates, napkins, and utensils. Plates were passed for Carrie to fill, and Snow brought out his gift of Jenk's Best whiskey. Carrie pretended to disapprove, and the doctors felt at home as they tucked into chicken seasoned with salt, red pepper, paprika, a pinch of sugar, and fried golden in butter with a little salt pork.

Part way through a chicken leg, Ben Elliott turned to peer into trees shrouding the exit from Snow's Rest Road. Being younger, Elliott heard the mule-drawn wagon first. It emerged out of shadows with three grim-faced men. Snow didn't know if he was more surprised to see Josiah and Buddy Jenks, or Sheriff John Wesley Freeman.

Standing, walking down the steps, and crossing the yard, Snow sorted how to begin from where to begin. Carrie called after him, "We still have plenty of chicken for everyone, and there's a peach pie."

Snow began with, "Good afternoon. You are in time to join our picnic." The three nodded and tipped hats in Carrie's direction.

Buddy started explaining, "We're here on serious..." and was cut off by Sheriff Freeman's raised hand.

Loud enough for those on the porch to hear, Freeman called, "Pleased to join you.", and continued quietly to Snow with, "Lucky for me I found both you and James Miles together. Save me some time." Freeman removed Snow's letter from the inside pocket of a jacket that lay across his lap and leaned over in Snow's direction. "Four young lads in a crabber hailed me at the mouth of St. Mary's River and gave me this letter. They were disappointed to be robbed of a sail to Leonardtown. I left them debating whether to claim another dollar from you."

Snow nodded and smiled imagining the scene. "Well, it's a good thing they found you. They were supposed to deliver the letter in person and return with an answer. So, it looks like you're the answer, and I owe them that dollar." The Sheriff stepped down from the wagon, and the Jenks tended their mules while Freeman and Snow walked away along the woods.

Freeman lowered his voice and turned his back toward the porch and wagon. "This has been my big week for letters. A Pinkerton agent sent me one from Baltimore with a story cut from the Baltimore Sun. Seems he doesn't think we

Linda A. Stewart

get any newspapers down here. He is looking for that new doctor, Elliott, with questions about a nurse reported missing up there. That Elliott on the porch?" Snow nodded.

Freeman lowered his voice to a whisper. "Is the body in Snow's Run the nurse he sent for?"

Snow shrugged. "Could be the nurse. Could be someone else."

Freeman nodded his understanding, turned toward the porch, and raised his voice. "Well, I am hungry as a brown bear at a bee hive and delighted to accept Mrs. Darberry's invitation." He gave the Jenks brothers a firm look, and they fell to silence.

With the mules unhitched, watered, and noses tucked contentedly in feedbags, the newcomers washed off the day's travel at the backyard pump and joined the picnic. By the time they reached the porch, it was evident from the look on Mile's face that

Carrie had revealed the secret in Snow's Run. She retreated into the kitchen. Dr. James Miles sat stock-still, a man counting between lightning bolt and thunderclap, considering the proximity of disaster. Elliott's wicker chair protested under his restless shifting, scraping the floor as he pushed back from the group. He was already standing when Snow introduced him to Sheriff Freeman. Bustling back from the kitchen with three additional plates, she filled them and refilled the others, slowing conversation, giving them all time to think.

Looking to Snow, Freeman picked up a chicken leg and started with, "Will, let's have you tell us about the body in Snow's Run."

Snow told of finding her, kept it brief, just the unembellished facts, as he would appreciate having them in his courtroom.

"So, who do you think she is?"

Snow thought, "She could be, might be, probably was Hattie whose body had never been found after the sinking of a sloop she and Piano Paul fled in following Richard Darberry's murder at Paul's hands." But, he said, "From what I saw, all I know is the body is probably a woman."

"You didn't see more than a boot and a foot?" Snow shook his head.

Pausing in the consumption of his chicken leg, Freeman eyed Elliott whose plate went untouched.

In spite of Freeman's previous scowl of disapproval, Buddy Jenks jumped into the void with, "There was a woman, young, thin but dressed nice. She got off the *Northumberland*. Passengers get off to stretch their legs, settle their stomachs sometimes. There was a bit of a swell that day. This woman and a tobacco buyer, a timber agent, and a few other passengers walked around while my order for the store got unloaded. So, then I picks up delivery ice and piles sawdust over it. But, this woman is still there. She had bags with her, a carpetbag and a black doctor's bag. Said she was a nurse. There wasn't nobody waiting for her. So, she was upset. She left on foot up Brome's Wharf Road."

Slack-jawed and wide-eyed, Elliott slowly turned his gaze toward Buddy Jenks. Freeman asked, "Who was supposed to be waiting for her?"

"She said a doctor. So, I thought she meant Dr. Miles. I told her to wait. If he didn't come, I'd get someone to take her, or take her myself. She asked directions to Bluestone Farm. So, I'm looking down the wharf out towards Brome's Wharf Road. I tell her it's to the right. She's lookin' at me. So, she looks over her right shoulder. But that's my left. It was the wrong way. So, she walked the wrong way. I thought I'd catch up with her when I got going with my deliveries. I never did see her again."

Freeman snapped, "When was that?"

"Last week in July. First week I delivered ice."

Elliott blurted out. "That's too early. Nurse Snareborn was due to arrive on the first Wednesday in August, August fifth." Silence fell hard on his outburst.

"What I mean is Nurse Dorothea Snareborn agreed to come to St. Mary's for private duty nursing, but did not arrive. A letter from the Private Duty Nursing Service at the University Of Maryland School Of Nursing said she would be here on Wednesday, the first week of August. She would have arrived with a black medical bag to use in community nursing."

"You have that letter?" Freeman was sharp. Miles sat up, looking defensive. Freeman raised his hand, nodded in capitulation, and backed off some.

Elliott shot a look of gratitude toward Miles and answered, "Yes. Furthermore, the day is getting late. Light will be waning along that run. If our actual purpose here is to exhume this woman, I will get my bag, and we will get on with it."

Ignoring Freeman's raised hand, indicating he should sit, Elliott strode off the porch toward Mile's carriage to retrieve his medical bag. Not being above a little defiance themselves, the Jenks brothers grinned and followed Elliott to retrieve shovels from their wagon. Miles shrugged, leaned back sipping his whiskey and smiled at Freeman. Freeman grinned back and finished his chicken.

Snow missed out on the revolt of Elliott and the Jenks, as well as Miles' and Freeman's amusement. On hearing the name Snareborn, he had left the back porch to retrieve a copy of the *Baltimore Sun* that came off the steamer *Northumberland* when it docked at Brome's Wharf. Lately, he kept his copies in the upstairs library, arranged by date to keep abreast of events in the outside world.

Freeman met Snow's questioning look with, "We let the younger men go ahead to do the hard work." Nodding at the paper in Snow's hand, he added, "I've read that article in the paper. James might have missed it." Wiping her hands on a tea towel, Carrie stepped out from the house kitchen into developing afternoon shadows on the back porch.

"This was in the *Baltimore Sun*, Friday, August seventh. I remembered it because Jane and I lived on East Hamilton Street when I was getting started in my law practice. Also, it isn't that unusual for a bride who has changed her mind to disappear or run away with another man. So, I wondered why this case was getting so much attention. As I remember it, Thomas Coode brought me this copy on Tuesday, August eleventh when he came for a visit." Then Snow read aloud.

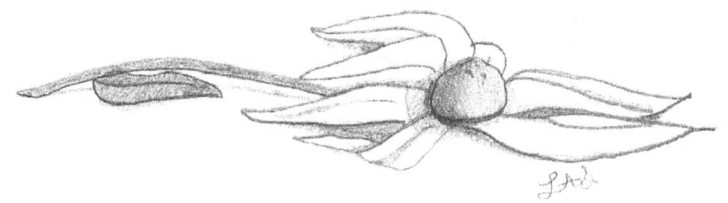

SOCIETY GIRL GONE MISSING

Miss Dorothea Rebecca Snareborn of East Hamilton Street Has Been Missing Since July 23rd

SHE WAS TO BE MARRIED

Had Good home with Relatives and No Reason to Disappear---Claimed to be Visiting Friends

Miss Dorothea Rebecca Snareborn, 20 years old, lives at the home of her sister and brother-in-law, Mr. and Mrs. James L. Critchen of East Hamilton Street. On Thursday, July 23rd, Miss Snareborn left for a seven-day visit to friends and did not return for her planned twenty-first birthday celebration on August second.

Miss Snareborn is engaged to be married to Mr. Gerald Ernest Rolands on August 30th

When Miss Snareborn did not return from the planned visit, her brother-in-law, Mr. James L. Critchen, grew more and more apprehensive over the young woman's prolonged absence. He reported her missing to authorities on August fourth."

Snow looked up at Freeman with raised eyebrow. "So, she was missing for at least a week before the brother-in-law contacted the police?"

Freeman nodded. "Don't know who he contacted first. Maybe the police. Maybe the Pinkertons. Might not have been a planned visit with friends. Nurse Snareborn accepted an assignment from some private nursing service. She was to work for Dr. Elliott, or so she told the service. A Pinkerton agent and the fiancé are arriving down to Leonardtown this

Wednesday on the *Calvert*. Lookin' to find Dr. Elliott. The Pinkerton is making all kinds of demands." Freeman's brow darkened. Snow and Miles waited, but Freeman made no additional revelations.

Chapter 6: A Body At Rest

Death is a Dialogue between
The Spirit and the Dust...
The Spirit turns away
Just laying of evidence
An Overcoat of Clay.
    Emily Dickinson (1830 – 1886)

Abruptly standing and pushing his chair away from the table, James Miles addressed Snow. "I'm thinking the young and overconfident may or may not have found the deceased by now. Why don't you lead us to where she is at rest before they overly disturb her?"

Sheriff Freeman organized the expedition. "We'll need a pail, some line, canvas tarp, and some wide solid boards for a pallet. Buddy took shovels with him from Jenks' wagon, but I'd rather have a hoe and a trowel or two."

After gathering Freeman's requests, the three headed into the woods along the path between Snow's Rest and Cawsin Farm. They were unaware that Carrie followed at a distance, gathering wild flowers and mint in a basket as she went.

Upon arrival within sight of Cawsin Farm, Freeman paused in amazement at the ruin of the place and turned to Snow with a frown.

Dr. Miles enlightened Freeman with, "Jane Cawsin Snow's parents passed away with consumption. Some of the worst cases I ever attended. Arsenic in Fowler's solution, creosote with codeine, and later heroine held off the pain, but in the end, all we could do was hope to relieve their suffering." It was all the explanation required at a time when dread of the disease left people reluctant to occupy a house where tuberculosis had spread to multiple family members.

Turning south, they followed the embankment to where it wandered across the spring. They found the toppled remains of Snow's childhood fort and the body in the Run. The three younger men were nowhere in sight but could be heard working their way up the Run from its mouth. Snow and Freeman let themselves down over the bank splashing into the stream.

When James Miles sat on a fallen tree trunk to catch his breath, Snow realized they would need Dr. Elliott. "James, I think the Jenks brothers are digging at the wrong overhang closer to St. Mary's River. Josiah saw me there when he came to visit yesterday. Could you walk down and herd them in this direction?"

As Miles stood and started down the Run toward its mouth, Snow noticed Carrie for the first time standing secluded in trees. With her lips pressed together, she met his surprised look with a disapproving stare. So there it was, the last of yesterday's deceptions revealed. He had seen the Josiah alone. The Run gave up one more secret like all the others.

Freeman saved him with, "Are you going to dig today or tomorrow?" Snow bent down and began clearing away mud, one trowel full at a time, from the now exposed legs.

Putting her basket down, Carrie took out cheese cloth and fistfuls of wild mint. After sprinkling mint in the middle of a yard long strip of cloth, she folded it over twice creating a gauze mask. She made another and approached the overhang where Snow and Freeman excavated through cloying clay and sand, exposing a decaying corpse.

"Sheriff Freeman, you might like this cheese cloth and mint mask tied around your mouth and nose." On her knees, Carrie inched toward the edge, but Snow climbed up to intercept her.

"As you told me yesterday, this is a dangerous task. Please stay away from the edge. Thank you for thinking of the masks." Although she nodded, her pressed lips told him to except only a temporary truce.

The Sheriff asked, "Do you think Mrs. Darberry should be here? This could be difficult for her."

Snow was quick to respond in his judicial voice while still facing Carrie. "Mrs. Darberry should be here if she wants to. And, we need her." Freeman shifted his stance, started to respond, but abandoned the argument. Carrie nodded her appreciation and retreated to sit on a fallen tree. Masks in place, they continued to dig carefully so as not to damage the corpse.

On the Run's northern shore, an expansive swoop of slate gray wings settled along the water's edge. After rustling her feathers into place like a judge arranging her robes, the great blue heron stared at the men through stern black eyes, weighing their intent.

Eventually, James Miles returned with the Jenks and Elliott. On Miles' insistence, the younger men shoveled down to the corpse from the top of the bank, eliminating the danger of entrapment under another collapse. When the Jenks dug into a layer of dense clay just above the corpse, Freeman and Snow took over again with trowels under Dr. Elliott's supervision. Mild scent of decaying vegetation strengthened to the nauseating stench of rotting flesh. Chilled spring water seeped from the embankment, washed over their hands, and over the corpse to reveal her last posture. With her back against the bank, she sat legs extended, hands palm outward over her eyes, jaw open in her last gasp or a final scream. Overwhelmed by this petrified moment of death, her liberators paused and watched escaping streams of water coiled over her face.

Taking charge, Sheriff Freeman reached for her right arm holding it gently, then worked his other hand behind her shoulder and down her back to support her. Snow held her left arm and supported her shoulder with his right elbow while placing his right hand behind her head. Ben Elliott placed his arms under her hips and legs. At a nod from Freeman, they lifted her out onto a tarp covered pallet of lashed boards. Wet, exhausted, and panting in the heat, they stepped back and sat on fallen tree trunks along the stream. While rinsing his hands in creek water, Snow realized the clay encrusting them was streaked with black. Carrie handed down a mason jar of fresh well water. They passed it around and rested in the shade.

After catching his breath, Elliott crept forward and spilled double handfuls of water over her hands, over her silt covered face. Pulling the hands away, he paused, winced, and shook his head. He loosened remaining clots of clay and stared closely at what remained of her features. After removing clods of mud from the dark, gray dress front, he felt around the neck and collar but found nothing. Deep furrows of worry fell from his face as he gasped a sigh of relief and returned to sit with the others. While continuing to stare at her, he shook his head answering some silent question.

Lowering themselves into the Run, the Jenks brothers wrapped and tied the unidentified woman to her pallet. The others joined them, and they lifted her out of her anonymous murky underworld into the light.

Silence took up watch over them all, a sentinel guarding against fear, leaving each to private thoughts of death. Across Snow's Run, the heron lifted into a glide upstream, judging the exhumation with several harsh croaks punctuated with snaps of her spear-like bill. At that moment, the moment when waning day sights the approaching night, air stood still and leaves hung limp in late afternoon heat like heads bowed in mourning. Carrie stepped forward with her Bible and wildflowers retrieved from her basket.

Snow displayed his clay smudged, sandy hands. Carrie gave the Bible to Dr. Miles, who held it closed in his hands and considered the circled mourners of differing faiths.

"Lord, we are gathered here today as your instrument to return Your lost child to the bosom of her family. Give us strength to do our best by her in Your name. Let us pray in silence."

Hands folded, some making the sign of the cross. Heads bowed. After a few moments, Miles led the communal 'Amen'.

Carrie stepped closer, placed wild flowers next to the body, took a searching look, met Snow's eyes, and shook her head. Snow nodded his agreement.

Freeman followed their silent communication with, "It isn't her, isn't Hattie Wells?"

Snow answered, "No. Mrs. Darberry and I are certain this is not her. Although the face is partially crushed, we can still see this is not Hattie."

Carrie interrupted, "Those are not her clothes."

"Based on what you know of her clothing, you are certain this isn't Hattie Maud Wells?"

"Yes, but even more, these are not this woman's clothes. The cut and cloth are good quality, but they don't fit her. Her figure is a much smaller size."

Sheriff Freeman turned to Elliott. "Did the body shrink in all that clay?" Dr. Elliott crouched and examined the corpse by ladling more water over her face, hands, and feet.

Miles broke in with, "John, you know as well as I that bodies first swell in decomposition. Mrs. Darberry has a good point. Something isn't quite right here."

Elliott argued. "There is slight decomposition, not enough except for the one foot exposed from under the collapsed stream bank. This cannot be the body of a woman dead for almost three weeks."

Freeman crouched next to Elliott, getting a better look. "You are saying this is not Dorothea Snareborn who arrived on the steamer *Northumberland* last week in July?"

"I only met Dot Snareborn once at a crowded commencement reception, so I can't be sure, but this woman can't be a woman dead for three or four weeks."

Buddy Jenks leaned in over them. Freeman raised an eyebrow. "Is this the woman who disembarked at Brome's Wharf the last week in July?"

Linda A. Stewart

Buddy nodded. "Yup. Sure is. Her hair was that color. I remember that dress. My wife would like a dress like that, all lace down the front and a layered skirt. But, I didn't see how any woman could walk to Bluestone Farm in it. And, she was wearing a fancy Sunday hat and white gloves."

Elliott shook his head again, but Miles broke in with, "One of my father's tenants buried hogs infected with cholera next to a tobacco barn and didn't tell anyone. Years later, another tenant tried to build a tobacco stripping shed against the barn. When he uncovered the hogs, they looked recently buried. They were packed deep in clay where no air or flies ever got to them."

Elliott regarded him with disbelief. Placing a hand on Elliott's shoulder, Miles smiled. "They don't teach you everything in medical school."

Carrie interrupted again. "She has a ring on her right hand. Does she have any other jewelry?" Elliott ladled more water over her hands.

John Freeman removed the ring, rinsed it in the pail, and passed it to Carrie. "What can you tell us about this ring?"

"First, I can tell you it was on her right hand, not on her left where an engagement ring is usually worn." After a thoughtful examination, Carrie added, "The story in the Baltimore Sun called her a 'society girl'. This should be a modern diamond engagement ring but this is an older ring. There are four settings for stones in this ring. The first is a blue-green lapis lazuli. The second missing stone was an opal. Opals crack and break easily. The last two are of different green shades. They are vermarine and emerald. The first letters of these stones spell L O V E. It's an old engagement ring, maybe from just after the War, and it was on her right hand. It was her mother's or grandmother's ring. This girl was not engaged to anyone."

Elliott nodded at Carrie's analysis before adding his observation. "Her left hand is blistered, possibly burnt. Skin and flesh of this girl's left hand are deteriorated far beyond the right hand, and the back of the sleeve is burnt."

"Girl?" Freeman frowned.

Carrie assured him. "Yes. She's young, very young and slight, I think. If I were sewing for her, I would never have placed those darts in that bodice to tailor it for this girl."

While Carrie informed the group of men on the subject of engagement rings and women's tailoring, Elliott reexamined the corpse. Pressing his fingertips methodically along legs, torso, arms, and shoulders, he discovered her history.

"Still, Dr. Elliott, you said you did go to Brome's wharf looking for her." The Sheriff persisted.

"Not the week that Buddy Jenks saw her. The letter said a nurse would come the first Wednesday in August."

Buddy interjected, "Dr. Elliott was at the wharf the second Wednesday after I started delivering ice. That would be the first Wednesday in August. He was waiting when the *Northumberland* docked. He went on board, and then he left alone."

While Buddy recited this history, Dr. Elliott retrieved a stethoscope and atomizer from his bag. First, he collapsed the bulb of the atomizer and used it to siphon out the corpse's one undamaged nostril. Taking up the stethoscope, he listened to the woman's lungs while slowly pumping her chest. He ran his hands across her chest, down her arms and legs again, feeling with his fingertips.

Finally, he announced, "There is congealed blood in her nostril but no gurgling of water in her lungs. This victim didn't drown. In addition, there is evidence of old, healed skeletal fractures that never received medical treatment. There is definite displacement and angulation in the left humerus three inches above the elbow. Also, there are indications of repeated right clavicular fractures, the kind you see more often in children if they don't drink enough milk."

Dr. Miles inquired, "Any indication of mandibular fracture?" Elliott shook his head.

Sheriff Freeman interrupted, "So at some time, she had a broken arm and broken collar bone that healed wrong but no broken jaw. Whoever he is, he hit her in the arm and shoulder where it didn't show?"

Then Elliott turned the anonymous woman over on her side, revealing her back and exposing a deeply carved gash at the base of her skull. Turning her further, he uncovering scorching up the underside of her left sleeve and across the back of her dress bodice. Snow looked down at his hands, remembered black streaks in clay and lowered himself into the Run to scrub them with sand.

In a tone of frustration, the Sheriff summarized the situation. "So, let's see what we have here. This young woman is dead, her body resting under an embankment in Snow's Run. We don't believe she looks like Hattie Maud Wells, who is still missing. She may or may not be Nurse Dorothea Snareborn. She arrived on the *Northumberland* on the last Wednesday in July carrying a black medical bag. The woman, or girl, Judge Snow found buried here shows signs of broken bones. She is wearing a ring that may or may not be an engagement ring. She now lies here with a wound on the back of her head, burns up the back of her dress, and she didn't drown. Eliminating the impossible, whatever remains, however improbable..." Freeman paused.

Elliott continued for him, "...must be the truth."

Freeman smiled at Elliott, amused to find a fellow fan of Arthur Conan Doyle, and finished with, "So, what remains?"

After a fleeting smile in Freeman's direction, Elliott responded with, "Perhaps we are supposed to think she was Nurse Dorothea Snareborn, but she is not."

"Or, she was a substitution, and Dr. Elliott was supposed to accept her." Dr. Miles conjectured.

Josiah speculated. "Whoever she is, she was bashed in the back of her head. Then she got too close to a fire. Someone chased her. Then she jumped or fell into Snow's Run and got crushed when the overhang collapsed."

Losing patience, Carrie brought speculation to an end. "We don't know what happened to her bags, her hat, or her gloves. We don't know how she got all the way over here from Brome's Wharf or who she met along the way. We don't know enough about her yet. There's no sense in all this guessing. For now, we are her only mourners."

At this point, Snow took over. "We will know if she is Miss Snareborn when her fiancé and the Pinkerton agent arrive on Wednesday to make an identification. Until then, we will place her in the springhouse. If Josiah and Buddy will go for ice, we can wrap her in a tarp and bury the ice under, over, and around her. There are enough reliable Miles cousins with good hunting hounds to keep raccoons and opossums out of the springhouse overnight." James Miles agreed to arrange a guard.

An owl hoot haunted through early evening as darkness tumbled from dense woods onto dusky fields. Each mourner went about his assigned task to place the unfortunate and anonymous woman in the springhouse where she lay, a body at rest.

Chapter 7: A Tale of Two Quilts

The Past is such a curious Creature
To look her in the Face
A Transport may receipt us
Or a Disgrace –
  Emily Dickinson (1830 – 1886)

Three quilts draped the pantry icebox that cradled block ice meant to protect the body at rest, meant to delay the decaying progress of time. Snow and Carrie discussed a plan to move that ice to the springhouse while sipping the last of Monday morning's Maxwell House.

Young Miles cousins who had stood watch at the springhouse through the night came for breakfast when they smelled smoke from the summer kitchen. They devoured a tray of Carrie's fresh ham biscuits, gulped down three pots of coffee, and returned to the springhouse forgetting to take fresh ice.

After finishing morning chores, Snow and Carrie crunched refried day-old biscuits with scraps of yesterday's chicken and stared at the icebox.

Carrie ran her hand over the uppermost quilt, picked off pieces of lint, and announced, "This is a Baltimore album quilt."

A precise pattern of blocks ran in a progression of flags, eagles, laurel wreaths, ships under sail, horns of plenty and cannons. It reflected a presumption of power and certainty in the universe. Appliqued and embroidered by a meticulous hand, it displayed craft raised to the level of art. The violet Turkey reds of common madder root complimented the deep blue-purple of indigo. The fast dark black of tropical Logwood and the grey-greens of Bayberry contrasted with the earthy yellow-brown ochre of iron-oxide pigment.

This lush coverlet echoed the affluent and comfortable life of its creator.

Carrie traced the patterns with her fingers while Snow finished his last biscuit. Together, they gently lifted the lavish construction folding colors into and under a thin homespun backing. Carrie ran her hand over the backing and commented, "This backing and the batting beneath have cotton seed caught up in the weave. No one ginned this cotton. Album quilts are usually signed. I can't find an embroidered signature, not even initials. Do you know how long this had been in your family?" Snow shrugged.

Carrying the quilt to Jane's sitting room, Snow unfolded it across the grand piano and peered closely at each block for clues to its origin. He examined the six flags of differing design that ran diagonally down through six rows of blocks from upper left to the lower right corner, one flag in each row. Each flag sported a unique number of stars, starting with the Betsy Ross flag of thirteen stars in a circle reflecting equality for each state. The second-row flag of fifteen stars, Francis Scott Key's Star Spangled Banner, was appliqued over bursts of cannon fire in Turkey red. Flags progressed from thirteen through fifteen, twenty, twenty-one, and twenty-three stars, ending with twenty-four. The last flag, the "Old Glory" of 24 stars, the flag of the Missouri Compromise, flew over a dove and olive branch. Snow searched for but found no signature.

He answered Carrie's question with, "You are correct. There is no signature. From the number of stars in the last flag, this quilt was finished after 1822, but I can't say I remember seeing it before."

Carrie sniffed disapproval. "In that case, there's no excuse for homespun cotton backing with embedded cotton seed. Even in St. Mary's County, you could get ginned cotton by 1816, or at least by 1820."

Snow turned up the lower right corner, fingering the backing. "It has no signature and the backing is poor quality. Was it unfinished? Were the batting and backing added by someone else at a later time?"

Carrie took the corner from him, turning it over, examining top and bottom, counting stitches. "The top is quilted with six stitches per inch, but the batting is tacked to the backing. The backing is basted on with uneven, large stitching along the edges. There is fading down the right side. This quilt is like the unfinished spearhead you found. Someone died. If you don't remember seeing this quilt before today, might it be from Jane's family? Perhaps it was kept at Cawsin farm. You may find the quilter buried there sometime after 1822."

Snow examined the faded area and grasping Carrie's analytical mind. He was startled to find himself comparing her to his sweet Jane who was so different and yet appreciating Carrie for that difference.

Returning to the back pantry, they removed the second smaller and much faded quilt without comment. Pieced together by generations, the spontaneous construction of saved fabrics at hand revealed its humble origin. Faded indigos, pale red double pinks, and faint earthy tones of overdyed greens narrated a tale of need. Stripes, plaids, and calico fragments of varied shape and size deviated in many directions. Loosely basted to this coverlet, an austere patchwork backing consisted of faded homespun bits, a fabrication of chaos. Frayed on one edge and ending in an open incomplete row, the whole laid bare an unfinished testimony. Its construction echoed the erratic and hectic life of its creators. One day it would hang under glass and dim light while a queue waiting to view its ancient heritage. On this day, Carrie and Snow carried this faded and worn patchwork quilt to Jane's piano. Placing it over the quilt of flags, they noticed the tattered patchwork covered all but the faded right-hand side, the side of Old Glory, the last flag.

Staring at that flag, Snow's thoughts drifted to his family history. He spoke softly, looking to test Carrie's acceptance more than the facts. "Are we sure Hattie is not laying in the springhouse?"

After a pause, she nodded. "Yes. It's a disappointment not to have it over with, but no, that girl is not Hattie. You're not disappointed, are you?" She said the last more as an accusation than a question. He felt her stiffen beside him, thought about her words, 'secrets grow a tangle'.

So, he recited the history. "There is a memorial to my brother David in the family cemetery next to my parents' grave."

When Carrie frowned at the apparent change of subject, he reminded her. "The inscription gives David's death date as May 6, 1863. It happened at Chancellor's Run where I fought against Jeb Stuart's Third Brigade, David's unit. David's name disappeared from CSA roster rolls after May sixth."

"Yes, I know." Sympathy and the shared sorrows of a generation filled her eyes. Snow opened Jane's roll topped desk and retrieved the tintype photograph of David with his family taken years after David's desertion and flight to Texas. "I found this in a bible at Cawsin Farm in June."

Carrie shuttered in premonition as goose bumps prickling down her arms. She examined the tintype and stared into the eyes of David Horatio Snow seated for a family photograph in his later years, cane in hand. She turned it over and read the inscription aloud. "David Horatio Snow,

Annabelle Cawsin Snow, Addie Cawsin, and child."

Snow turned away, looked out windows into the distance; across his fields, across his river, across his world. With her hand on his arm, Carrie stepped to face him. "William, is this Hattie's Annabelle, Hattie's mother? Is it possible that Hattie is David's grandchild, and your grandniece?"

He shrugged. "Possibly. I don't know with any certainty. David is dead. They're all dead now. No one is left to tell their secrets." She moved her hand to his shoulder.

They both refrained from giving voice to the possibility there was one who still lived, one who knew. John Benjamin Lundy, the Snow brother's childhood slave companion, had disappeared in 1863 and reappeared years later. He became caretaker of Snow's Rest and father of

Piano Paul. She handed the tintype back, and Snow slipped it into the desk.

Snow started to leave the room, but she stopped him. "William, about the sleepwalking and the lantern, did you find that lantern in here one morning the week after I came?" He nodded.

"And, you thought I had written a letter and left the lantern on the piano? Or maybe, I was sleepwalking with a lit lantern?" He said yes and she resumed, "One night, the first week I was here, an odd tapping noise woke me. At first, I couldn't remember where I was. All the noises creeping around the Rest at night were still strange to me. I thought you were up and about in the middle of the night. I left my bed to see if you wanted some warmed milk." He smiled thinking he would have wanted something other than warm milk. She explained, "I was unfamiliar with the kitchen, and I stumbled against a chair in the dark. There was a light shining into the hall from this room, from the kitchen lantern left on this piano. The light went out, and I heard you go out to the front porch. The next morning you were angry about the lantern on the piano and the stationary. Do you think... I mean, did you get up that night?"

Truth floated into the room. Like a moth fluttering into the folds of Snow's reality, it ate holes into the certainty of his experience. In her eyes, he read the hope he would say yes, maybe he had been walking around the house in the night.

He shook his head. "No. With the amount of Melrose Rye I was drinking then, it was difficult enough to get up in the morning, never mind wander around the Rest in the night. I apologize for speaking harshly to you that morning. If I hadn't, you might have told me this sooner."

In the long pause hanging between them, the dinginess of Jane's music room pressed in on him. He became aware of faded curtains and yellowing pages of piano music. The bud vase was chipped and the linen dust cover thrown over a sewing machine was stained with black. Perhaps it was the black stain or the shape under the dust cover that caught his attention. Jane's sewing room was the converted, never occupied upstairs nursery. Lifting the cover, he found the 1878 Remington No. 2 typewriter his law clerk had convinced him to replace with a modern 1900 Underwood No. 5 only two years earlier. He tapped a few keys on the old cast off machine.

"Is this the sound, the tapping?" The expression of surprise on her face answered him. The corner of a discarded document appeared under the machine's carriage and Snow pulled it out. He read the first two lines of an unfinished letter aloud and looked up at Carrie. "So, Hattie was here. Well. Fortunately, you did not walk down the hall into Jane's music room.

She may still have that Colt revolver of mine." Carrie stared at the typewriter for a long moment, then hurried out of the room.

In the kitchen, he found her folding the third quilt. Before he could say more, they heard the creaking of wagon wheels from the back yard heralding the arrival of replacements for the Miles cousins. Carrie hurried to meet them with the remains of the coffee and handful of tin cups, but the Miles were uninterested. They started unloading equipment including tripods and a rough homemade coffin. Snow's sudden sharp order to leave everything in the wagon brought them to a halt.

At that moment, Dr. James Miles came into sight with Sheriff Freeman seated beside him under the shaded cover of a doctors carriage. Assessing the situation, Sheriff Freeman began with, "Judge Snow, I apologize for not arriving first to explain my plan." He paused to show his sincerity and went on. "We have a problem. We need to identify this unknown woman found dead along Snow's Run. As time passes, identification will become increasingly difficult. It has now become necessary out of respect for the dead to bury her before identification. Two of Dr. Miles's nephews have cameras with them. We will take photographs and bring the film to Leonardtown. Vernon King will develop it for us at the St. Mary's Beacon offices. Photographs will help her family with identification when, or even if, we find them."

Before Snow could respond, the trot of hoofs and crunch of wheels heralded yet another arrival. All heads turned to meet the kind but determined gaze of Father Francis from St. Ignatius as he descended for the parish buggy. Sheriff Freeman persisted, "Father Francis will be with us to supervise and will conduct a burial."

The arrival of the Jesuit brought an instantaneous change in tone. First Father Francis greeted Snow, warmly shaking his hand. As the two photographers unloaded their equipment, a competition to impress the priest developed between them.

Always interested in current developments, Father Francis first examined the 1900 Eastman Kodak folding pocket camera. The owner claimed it had the finest Rapid Rectilinear lens and would take pictures with less distortion. He displayed its sets for three stops and its reversible viewfinder. The owner then removed what looked like a shotgun shell from his pocket and demonstrated loading the camera in daylight with cartridge film. Then he explained it took $3\frac{1}{4}$ by $4\frac{1}{4}$ inch pictures with excellent detail and only cost $17.50.

Next, the Jesuit examined a small cardboard box camera with one lens on the side, one focal length, and named after a cartoon read in the Baltimore Sun Paper. The Brownie camera's owner bragged it took snapshots; photographs shot quickly without long exposure times. The Brownie cost only one dollar. The folding pocket camera owner countered that the Brownie camera only developed $2\frac{1}{2}$ inch pictures.

Smiling and lowering his voice, James Miles predicted Father Francis would own a Brownie camera before Christmas. They grinned in agreement. Miles went on, "I sent Ben Elliott out on house calls this morning. He is more shaken by this than he let on yesterday. Freeman is suspicious of him. That letter Elliott received from the Private Nursing Service said Nurse Dorothea Rebecca Snareborn would arrive on 'the following Wednesday'. It posted from Baltimore on Friday, July 24th. Elliott says he did not receive the letter until the next Thursday. That would be July 30th, the day after the Wednesday Buddy Jenks met a nurse at Broome's wharf. Mail being slow arriving at times, it's entirely possible. Elliott says that's why he showed up at the wharf the next Wednesday, August 5th, when Buddy saw him board the *Northumberland*. Elliott was supposedly searching for his nurse." Nodding in Freeman's direction, he added, "Sheriff Freeman is having difficulty believing him."

Freeman stood stone faced listening to the conversation. When Miles finished, the sheriff turned the conversation to the Pinkerton agent, a subject of some irritation to his way of thinking. "Sometime around Tuesday, I expect the fiancé, Gerald Rolands, to show up with two Pinkerton agents in tow. With the body already buried on Jesuit property and photographs hopefully available, there will be little reason for them to show up here." Snow and Miles expressed agreement with Freeman's attempt to limit the Pinkerton's investigation.

"However," Freeman continued, "if they do decide to come down for a visit, you might want to make Dr. Elliott unavailable and yourselves well-armed. Not that I think they'll bring a private army down here, but God only knows what they might be up to. If this woman is the nurse, then her brother-in-law is a manager of the Baltimore branch of the Pennsylvania Railroad and reports to Leonor F. Loree, the new company president. The fiancé, Roland, works directly under the brother-in-law. Railroads don't think they're above the law. They think they are the law."

They all knew the Pinkerton Agency's international involvement in the demise of various outlaws, including Robert Leroy Parker, the infamous Butch Cassidy. Snow had more than passing thought that Dr. Elliott might be in danger.

Snow reverted to judicial interrogation. "Didn't you tell us the brother-in-law hired two agents? That isn't an army."

"The railroad hired one agent and a trainee from the Pinkerton agency's office in Baltimore at the brother-in-law's request. The agent's name is Frank P. Geyer."

Recognizing the name of the agent who tracked down the serial killer H. H. Holmes, Miles shot Freeman a look of alarm. Freeman continued, "So, this may be something bigger. With Geyer coming, they don't need an army."

While they were talking, Father Francis had brought the group together for prayer. After making it clear this was the beginning of a burial that would take place on property belonging to the Jesuit Order, he organized the group. He nodded in Snow's direction but asked Carrie to lead him to the springhouse. So, they went into the woods led by the Jesuit with his Bible, and Carrie Francis Darberry, a hand tatted shawl draped over her head, her rosary in hand, and the third quilt folded over her arm.

At the springhouse, the solemnity of their situation settled over the group as they became mourners for a woman none had ever met in life. Both photographers quietly asked the body be removed from shade to brighter light farther down Snow's Run toward St. Mary's River. The Jesuit agreed and told both photographers they could take six exposures each. Photographs taken in respectful silence to assure her identification included photographs of injuries to assure her justice.

As they watched the process, Snow stepped closer to Sheriff Freeman. "This morning I found an unfinished letter you will need to see before talking to Detective Geyer." Freeman only raised his eyebrows and nodded.

Carrie unfolded the third quilt, the quilt with diagonal rows of four squares set on point and looking like the steps of a ladder. She spread it in the coffin to accompany the unknown. Then the victim's poll bearers lifted her into the coffin and folded the tattered quilt over her. They buried her shrouded in the only example of a pre-war, Jacob's ladder pattern ever found and now lost.

Father Francis led her mourners in prayer.

"God our Father,
Your power brings us to birth,
Your providence guides our lives,
And by Your command, we return to dust."

Snow's thoughts focused on dust; the dust collecting over Jane's possessions at Snow's Rest, the dust settling over generations of quilters, the dust covering the tale of the two quilts draping Jane's piano.

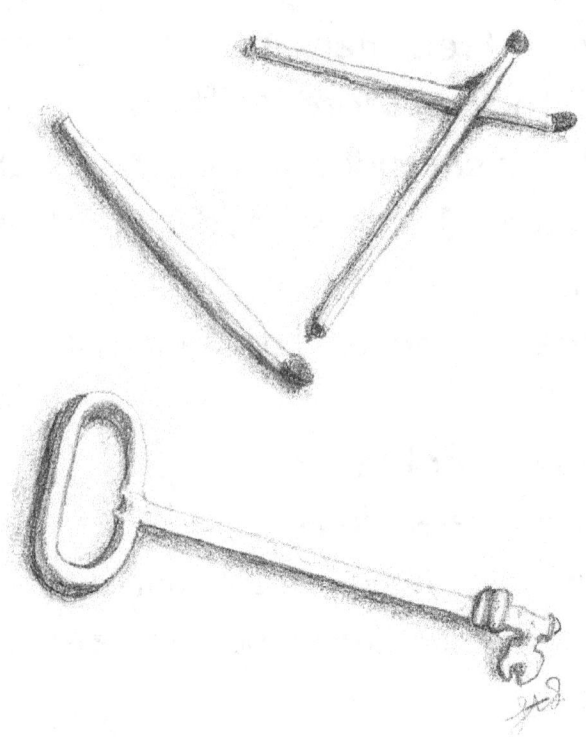

Chapter 8: The Key

Slipping new brass keys
Into rusty iron locks and
Shouldering till at last
The door gives and
We are in a new room...
  Carl Sandburg (1878 – 1967)

Snow was surprised to find a key inserted in his father's gun cabinet lock, a key identical to the one in his hand. Surprised to find two keys, he was also surprised he had left one in the lock. He opened the unlocked cabinet door.

With most of his firearms removed to Baltimore, Snow's family collection arrayed his Druid Park Terrace library walls. The early rifles made for interesting conversation among Baltimore gentlemen who rarely found occasion to use them outside of an infrequent hunt in the country.

One piece, a flintlock, muzzle loading Harper's Ferry Model 1803, the first rifle made by an American armory, charmed them all. Allegedly used by Snow's grandfather in defense of the Rest during the War of 1812, it was quite popular with Snow's attorney and banking colleagues. After a few rounds of Melrose Rye, they enjoyed hefting its nine pounds, sighting down its 33-inch barrel, and imagining the whip-snap of its single shot. Snow always suspected his grandfather had the common sense to retreat inland for the safety of his family when the British were raiding along the Chesapeake. Scorched timbers, found buried in the back walls of the Rest, were a mute testimony to his ancestor's wise retreat. However, the legend of resistance with the flintlock, muzzle loader created a grander tale.

Snows Run

An amusing story revolved around the Remington Rider single shot parlor pistol. Snow's mother, Anna Maud Snow, kept it by her bedside during what she called 'The War Between The States'. The .17 caliber, silver plated on brass toy with a three-inch barrel fired a powderless, percussion cap fulminate charge. It was nowhere near the weapon the rifle-barreled, .44 caliber, walnut stocked, single shot derringer Booth used to assassinate Lincoln. Nevertheless, one morning his mother had fired it at the cook who woke her out of a sound sleep delivering the breakfast tray. The incident resulted in the cook refusing to deliver breakfast beyond the upstairs hall table. Snow's father removed himself to his library couch to avoid a heart attack until his wife agreed to give up her weapon.

Removed from the lock, the second key revealed few marks of wear. After years of enduring Snow's amusing story of Anna Maud's derringer, Jane searched for this second key. She used it to removed Snow's .41 caliber Remington Model 95 double barreled derringer from the gun cabinet. Before Snow came down for the summer, she slept alone. So, Jane kept the weapon by her bed. Sarah, their cook housekeeper, took to hailing the house and waiting for an answer before entering each morning. On his arrival from Baltimore, Snow had insisted the derringer return to the cabinet. This morning, he searched the cabinet, but the derringer wasn't there. He assumed Jane had removed it sometime last summer. So, where had she hid it this time?

From the firearms remaining at the Rest, Snow selected a .31 caliber, 1861 Colt Pocket Police Revolver. He opened the green velvet lined case, removed the gun, and searched for a cleaning rod as he couldn't recall the last time the revolver had been cleaned. The bulging uneven topline and stubby 4-inch barrel made the blue gunmetal weapon less than elegant, but it remained his father's favorite. With its weight under two pounds, its less than 9-inch length easily fit in an inside coat pocket unnoticed. Inaccurate after 20 yards or so, it was a defensive weapon. Snow took it, case and all, locked the gun cabinet door, and placed one key on his key fob. He hid the newer key behind his 1891 first edition of Ambrose Bierce's Tales of Soldiers and Civilians and went down to breakfast.

Placing the pocket revolver case on the back porch table, Snow strolled out to a cloudless morning. Sunlight embraced the day as he crossed to the summer kitchen anticipating his tin cup of coffee. He hoped for a plate of bacon and eggs with perhaps some ham and fried potatoes. A three-pound rasher of bacon at .14 per pound and a ten-pound corned ham at .12 per pound were among the scant supplies Snow purchased along with a block of ice at

Broome's Wharf store after Monday's funeral. As he usually returned to Baltimore before the end of September, his purchase was meager. With Carrie planning to join the Miles' household and Elliott's practice, Snow had yet to solve issues around closing the Rest without a caretaker.

Snow's 'Good morning.' met with a nod and an echo like response. Carrie stood, back to him, in a faded farm dress and frayed apron, her hair tightly braided into a coil. One soiled plate and fork soaked in a galvanized wash tub next to the stove. Placing her coffee cup on the side warmer, she handed Snow a plate of hoecakes in molasses with two strips of bacon. She picked up her cup, but made no move to join him at breakfast. After a pause, he turned to walk back toward the porch but stopped abruptly when she spoke. Over her shoulder, she informed him she would sail her small catboat upriver to Darberry Farm this morning.

Recalling Carrie's ineptitude under sail, Snow returned and stood beside the stove, facing her. "Your boat..." When, finally, she looked up, he continued,"... hasn't been away from the dock in several weeks, not since the Jenks sailed it down here for you. Would you like me to check it out before you leave?" He wanted to ask when she was returning but thought better of it.

"No, I'll be fine." Reading his mind, she explained, "I'll only be gone for part of the day. I will be back in time to cook your dinner. Buddy Jenks is thinking of leasing my place, and I want to clean it up some before he shows it to Sissy." Shadows under her eyes revealed a restless night redolent with decision.

"I see. If you wait until I finish morning chores, I could go with you to help." When she shook her head, he pressed on with, "While we don't know for certain Hattie

Wells has left the area, you really shouldn't go anywhere alone."

Carrie pursed her lips. "Hattie is gone. That scrap of a letter you found under the typewriter was only her first attempt at a fraudulent recommendation. She finished it, here or somewhere else, and is far away as nurse Annabelle Cawsin Wells by now. What did Sheriff Freeman think of the letter? Does John Freeman thinks she's still here? Does he plan to search for her?"

Surprised she knew Freeman had seen the letter, Snow shook his head. "Freeman doesn't think it is evidence related to the disappearance of Miss Dorothea Rebecca Snareborn. I showed it to Elliott as well. He said the letter heading is correct, and Mrs. Katharine A. Taylor is, in fact, Superintendent of Nurses at the University Of Maryland School Of Nursing. If Hattie is still here somewhere and needs to finish that letter, either one of us could come into the house and surprise her at it."

Carrie turned away to remove a pan of the day's biscuits from the oven. "I examined the ink ribbon on the Remington typewriter. Jane must have replaced it with a new ribbon and not used it very often. You can look at the ribbon yourself. The words 'Sincerely Yours' are slightly visible just before Superintendent Taylor's name and title on the ribbon. Like you said. Sometime when we weren't here, perhaps on a Sunday, Hattie finished the letter and is gone."

Snow thought, "And now you will be gone, too. And perhaps your purpose in coming here was to find Hattie as much as to take care of me for Jane's sake, as you said." But, he said, "Well, give a holler if you need help getting underway." He hesitated, but she made no reply. Perhaps she was correct in her assumptions, but he would still carry the pocket pistol and lock the Rest up at night regardless of the heat.

Snow carried his breakfast to the back porch, ate, and cleaned the pistol. Carrie stood with her back towards him and scraped a cast iron frying pan. On the day of her arrival, she had said Jane would want a neighbor to look after him. From that day on, they had eaten breakfast together.

"There are few things lonelier than eating alone." she had said, and he thought, "Drinking alone."

Now, he attributed the distance in her behavior to their impending departures on separate paths; he to Baltimore, and she to Bluestone Farm. He remembered the feather light touch of her hand on his arm as they walked in the rose garden the day of her first visit. He remembered her flowering pink chintz along the darkly wooded path. He remembered the silken touch of hair against his hand as he removed the silver hairpin securing her pince-nez. He remembered the warmth and sympathy in her hand on his shoulder when he showed her David's photograph.

Eyes down and mouth set, Carrie hoisted the hot, cloth wrapped pan of biscuits across the yard. Snow recalled a description of Carrie told him by his wife's relations, the Overzee sisters. They had described Carrie as 'homely and sour', as having difficulty finding a husband until she had inherited property. Gaunt and tall, she trudged through the porch. Reflecting on her life of grief and hardship, he observed it etched onto her face and form. He heard her pump an inch of water into the deep sink before setting the pan to cool.

Sweet scent of Jane's summer roses wafted across the yard and through the porch reminding him of Jane's easy smile. With his breakfast abandoned, Snow placed the unloaded pistol with loose ammunition in a linen bag. Then, he walked out through the back and around the house rather than through the kitchen, on his way to morning chores.

Later, while finishing the milking with his forehead pressed to the Jersey's warm side, Snow felt the cow quit munching the forkful of timothy. She raise her head to stare out the barn and across the field. He stood and looked over her back. As he suspected, all the barn's creatures were watching Carrie walk down the road to the dock where her catboat drifted at the end of a line. Two large baskets hung heavy at her arms' length. A summer straw hat secured by a scarf flopped with each stride. Snow sat back down on the three-legged stool to strip the last drops of milk from the cow. He planned to finish chores before walking down to the Run and rescuing Carrie.

By the time he turned the cow out, Carrie had reached the dock and struggled to pull her little craft closer. Snow walked behind the barn to pump water into the pasture trough. As he did, Carrie lowered her baskets to the deck and climbed aboard. He failed to notice her cast off. She raise the lone sail and sculled the tiller back and forth to encourage her flat-bottomed craft out into the Run.

Surprised to find Carrie vanished from view when he glanced back toward the river, Snow wonder how she had managed to get up river and around Horseshoe Point so quickly. Abruptly, it occurred to him she had sailed or sculled up the Run's deeper side on her way to Cawsin Farm. He thought of trotting down to the dock to look up the Run, but she might be at the farm by now. Instead, he retrieved the linen bag from the barn and started up the hill towards the path in the woods, loading the pistol as he went.

Water in the upper Run ran shallow, even for a catboat. Carrie vigorously sculled her craft over the muddy bottom but could not get close enough to throw a line over pilings of Cawsin Farm's aging dock. First curious and then amused, Snow watched the futility of her several efforts from shaded seclusion before walking across the overgrown yard to assist her. Carrie sat down in defeat and waited for him to pick his way down the dock's remaining planks before throwing the line in his direction. It took three throws before she got it close enough for him to catch.

Surveying the bottom, he pulled the boat sideways towards deeper water before dragging it close enough for her to disembark. As she hoisted herself up the dock line, he knelt, reached down behind her with one arm, and stood pulling her up. Loose ends of her scarf fell open as she placed one arm around his shoulder. The hat tumbled, and she leaned back snatching it in mid-air. Snow wrapped both arms around her, hoisting her up off the boards. Though she was tall, he held her feet dangling above the dock, watched her blush, released her, and grinned boyishly as she slide out of his arms to regain her dignity. Carrie gave him a look that was half smile, half annoyance.

The humor of the moment pleased him. "Did you think I wouldn't notice your navigational error?"

She secured her straw hat, smoothed her dress and apron into place, but didn't answer his question. Instead, she responded with, "I am looking for something."

"Or someone?" He spoke sharply, abandoning humor.

She looked down at the loose boards of docking, then back up into his eyes. "Did you search Cawsin Farm for the missing hat and gloves or the nurse's bag?"

"No. There hasn't been time."

"Well, if those items can't be found, it will answer some questions. Especially in light of that letter's content."

He nodded, thought of repeating his warning against going about alone, but conceded to the apparent futility. "We'll search for them together."

When he slipped his hand under her elbow to guide her down the rotting pier, she pulled back. "I'll follow you." Smiling, she added, "You can fall through first." He grinned back.

After gingerly picking their way down the dock, they crossed the yard and stopped at the Cawsin family cemetery. He concurred when she said, "That Baltimore album quilt was beautifully stitched, but poorly finished. Surely the quilter is buried here."

They entered the family plot, stepping over collapsed and rusted iron fencing. Dutifully reading names and dates on moss covered stones, they left none out so that none would be forgotten. Dates on the grave of Jane's grandmother, Elizabeth Miles Cawsin, dates of 1798 to 1848, indicated she was most likely the quilter.

Snow followed Carrie's gaze as she looked across the yard in the direction of long ago vanished slave cabins. "The hands that finished it, the hands that stitched the other patchwork quilt, are out there somewhere. If Louisa Mae or Jane had finished the quilt of flags, they would have used ginned cotton."

"Maybe or maybe not. If the album quilt was backed before the war, then that might be true. If it was backed during the war, that might account for the poor quality of cotton. After the war, all of the Cawsin family slaves moved away, and some changed their names. Many of the Snow slaves changed their names as well, but some of them stayed to lease land and work the Rest. They probably finished that quilt when Jane and I lived in Baltimore."

"Yes, I remember." Former Cawsin farm slaves had left as a group after the War. Jacob Ezekiel Cawsin had gone to Orphan's Court with intentions of placing all children of his former slaves under guardianship. The guardianship amounted to continued servitude until they came of age. Snow's father, William Thomas Snow II, had freed his slaves just before the Emancipation Proclamation and protected those who stayed along with their families after the war. John, who married Sarah, was the last of that line, as Snow was the last of his. Carrie speculated, "Maybe those quilts were in the Cawsin farmhouse at the time Jacob and Louisa Mae died. It might account for the lack of wear, for how the quilts survived all these years."

Knowing Carrie referred to the gruesome deaths of Jane's parents from consumption, Snow agreed. No one would use a quilt that covered them during their illness. Snow turned toward the house, and Carrie followed.

They were on the back porch, about to enter through opened double doors that hung on loose hinges, when he heard it again and knew he had ignored it the first time. Not the trot or walk of the horse's hoof, but the stomp of a tethered horse secluded in the woods, a sound muffled by bird calls and rustling leaves. Barely audible, that stamp of hoof warding off flies preceded a snort of annoyance. Creak and jingle of harness followed as the animal shook to rid itself of pests.

While Snow and Carrie stood before the opened doors, an intruder's footfall above them spooked a cascade of nesting swallows aloft through a collapsed upstairs bedroom roof. Carrie stepped into the farmhouse ahead of Snow. He reached out for her elbow, pulled her back, and turned her away from the opening behind a door out of the line of fire. He pulled open the drawstring linen bag and stepped into the house, pocket pistol in hand. Upstairs floor boards creaked as heavy boot strides made their way from the master bedroom into the upper hall.

Snow called out, "Who's there?"

"Hello? Hello downstairs?" A man's voice, the voice of Dr. Bennett Augustine Elliott, preceded him down the stairs. Snow stepped through into the lower central hall. First, Elliott's legs and then his torso with empty hands at his side descended. Snow held the gun steady as Elliott stumbled in surprise and hastily retreated to the second-floor landing.

"Judge Snow, it's Dr. Elliott, Ben Elliott. Can I come down?"

Carrie stirred but retreated behind the door when, without turning his head, Snow abruptly pointed back at her with his free hand.

He demanded in a lowered voice, "Did you know he would be here?"

Exasperated, she whispered back. "No. I would have told you when you helped me tie up, and I saw you had the pistol. I wouldn't want you to shoot him."

To Elliott, he raised his voice, "What are you doing here in my house?"

"Sir, I apologize for trespassing. I'm looking for anything that will prove I didn't know that woman, anything that will explain what happened to Dot Snareborn. I'm not armed. Can I come down?"

"Yes." Snow lowered the pistol but kept it in hand. Elliott stepped down three stairs, leaned over to get a better look at Snow, and held his empty hands palms out.

After a long pause emphasizing his displeasure, Snow tucked the gun back into the linen bag slung around his shoulders but kept the bag's mouth open. Elliott eased himself half way down the stairs.

"I apologize for not getting your permission to search."

"What did you find?"

"So far, nothing that has anything to do with that nurse, but I couldn't get into the front parlor. The door's locked. I only just got up the stairs when those birds made all that racket, and you called from the center hall." Elliott continued cautiously down keeping his hands in front of him. "Sherriff Freeman doesn't believe me, doesn't believe I didn't know which day Dot Snareborn or that other nurse planned to arrive. I noticed this house through the woods the day we dug her out of the mud. It occurred to me she might have come here from Broomes Wharf."

"The woman who typed that letter is armed with a Colt revolver. If she was here..." Snow let the implication settle in on Elliott.

Blinking, Elliott. "And you thought I might be her?"

From behind Snow, Carrie spoke harshly to Elliott. "You told us that you only met Dorothea Snareborn once, but you call her

Dot. People don't use other people's nicknames unless they know them well. You are not completely truthful with us."

Elliott's shoulders sagged as he glanced away. "I met Nurse Snareborn when we were both in training. Mrs. Darberry, you were right about the engagement ring. Dot's engagement ring is a diamond. She carried it pinned under her collar when she was on the ward. Occasionally, she showed it to other nurses and nursing assistants. I think she made sure I saw it. The diamond was average size, about a quarter karat, but it was set with two smaller stones in white gold filigree. The wedding was to be sometime in August. She said sometime after her birthday. So, you can imagine my surprise when I got a letter announcing her impending arrival."

Snow inquired, "Then, you knew it was not her after we uncovered the body?"

"Yes. It was a relief and a shock at the same time." Elliott talked more to himself than Snow and stared at the locked front parlor door. Removing his hat, he wiped his brow with his sleeve. Snow's hand moved up to the linen bag.

"Do you know who the victim is?" Snow's stern tone brought Elliott back into focus. Seeing Snow's shift in stance, Elliott stumbled back up one stair.

"No, sir. That is, I'm not sure. She looks familiar, but if she were one of the nursing assistants or a first year nursing student, I wouldn't have spoken to her. I wouldn't have given her instruction directly. However, I have met that fiancé, Rolands." Irritation infused Elliott's tone. "Rolands used to arrive at the ward before the end of rounds and want to walk Nurse Snareborn home early. He made his displeasure with her chosen vocation obvious. Once, when he didn't show up at the end of evening rounds, I offered to pay for a taxi and escort her home myself. He arrived as I was putting Dot into the taxi and made unpleasant accusations. Dot told me that her sister had introduced them and promoted the engagement. Rolands works for the Pennsylvania Railroad, and the sister's husband is his boss."

Carrie interrupted, "But she kept up with her training even under pressure from the fiancé? She didn't quit because she was to be married?"

"I'm not sure she intended to go through with the wedding. Once at the end of rounds, when they were walking out ahead of me, Rolands said something about not putting up with another wedding postponement. Dot said she didn't need him making her decisions, didn't need him to support her."

Her doubtful tone evident, Carrie persisted, "Would she have been able to support herself as a nurse?"

"No. At least not in the same fashion. There is increasing demand for hospital trained private duty nurses. Doctors are pushing for trained nurses in postoperative critical care. There is a proposed bill in the General Assembly to establish the state's first nursing registration. Still, Dot was used to living well." Elliott's gaze wandered back to the locked front parlor door.

Snow interrupted. "The front parlor has been locked for years. No one can get in without forcing a window or picking the lock because the key is still in the room. Every time we broke in, the door ended up locked again, and the key ended up inside the room again." Noting Elliott's astonishment, he added, "Jane decided her parents didn't want the room disturbed after they were waked in it. The funeral was held in that room as well." With obvious agitation, he ended with, "Best to leave well enough alone."

Elliott stared incredulously at Snow. Carrie placed her hand on Snow's arm and spoke quietly. "William, there must be a second key somewhere in the house. Jane may have wanted to lock her bad memories away. If we are to make a thorough search of this house, we need to find the second key."

Snow nodded, dropped his hand from the bag's chord, and signaled Elliott to come down. Carrie began the search for the key in dust-covered furniture nearest the door, but the search of the house proved unproductive.

In time, with the futility of the quest, Snow suggested they investigate the summer kitchen. A heap of broken boards, it lay half crushed under a giant fallen oak. On their way towards the dilapidated structure, he explained that Hattie and Paul had rendezvoused there to avoid detection.

Snow remembered his brother, David, had done the same in an earlier time. A vision, a persistent dream, rose from Snow's childhood memory. Drifting through woods to the Cawsin farm kitchen house, spying on his older brother as little brothers do, he found David in the embrace of raised skirts and petticoats. Long bare legs opening in the dark drifted out of focus in his memory.

Carrie and Elliott were several steps ahead before they realized Snow had stopped and they turned to wait for him. Without explanation, he joined them and continued across the yard.

Acrid scent of damp ashes in a rusted stove lingered under the ramshackle remains of a roof. As their eyes adjusted to darkness under rubble, they observed mosquito netting hanging from nails in rafters and draped over old quilts that covered moldy straw bedding. Mentioning the scorching on the anonymous victim's dress, Elliott opened the stove's fire door and stirred around in ashes looking for anything.

Snow stood back, surveyed the debris, and spotted something white, something blown by wind under intruding branches of the ancient oak. Stooping, he crept forward, retrieved it, crawled back, and held out an open envelope addressed to Dr. Bennett Augustine Elliott. Elliott snatched at it expectantly before Snow could warn him it was empty. Elliott's disappointment was palpable. He sat on a discarded flour barrel, face in hands.

Carrie placed her hand on his shoulder. "You were hoping to hear from her, hoping she would come later?" Elliott nodded.

Carrie continued, "On the envelope, the handwriting, is it hers?" Elliott nodded again. Snow stared at Carrie's hand resting on Elliott's shoulder, remembered it on his own shoulder, remembered the solace of her touch.

Turning away, he walked toward the opened stove door and spotted the glitter of something on the floor. With his back to the others, he reached down and lifted a cigar cutter along with one paper cigar band from behind the stove foot. The band was embossed with a train engine and the words 'Moore's Imported Turkish', a brand not familiar to him. That was not a surprise as there were at least 500 cigar factories in Baltimore. More impressive was the double ended, silver cigar cutter that he slipped into the deep side pocket of his overalls to examine later. Leaning down to view ashes in the old rusted stove, he saw thin flakes of black left by burning paper, perhaps the remains of a letter. At one side, he recovered what appeared to be a small, melted button without a backing. Rolling it around in his palm, he walked back and held it out for Carrie's inspection.

"Only one?" she asked.

"I didn't find another."

"It's small enough to be a woman's glove button. All burned and melted like that, I can't tell the shape. There should be two or three."

Gazing at the stove, she walked toward and past it, searched around and behind it. On the stove mantle a few matches, some broken and some burnt, sat beside a tin matchbox. On impulse, she lifted and shook the matchbox. Metal clinked on metal. Prying it opened, she dumped the contents into her hand, contents including matches and a door key.

Chapter 9: The Opening Door

Life and death appeared to me ideal bounds, which I should first break, and pour a torrent of light into our dark world.
Mary Shelley (1797 – 1851)

They stood before the locked door, and she handed him the key. Hesitating, sensing possibilities within, he inserted the key and opened the door. As the rusting lock gave little resistance, and the bolt slid back effortlessly, a premonition swept over him. Snow pushed against the door with his left hand and held the revolver in his right, knowing they would find answers waiting in the dank front parlor. Only stale air and dust met them as the door creaked open.

While walking across the room to boarded up French doors leading to the veranda, Snow had an immediate sense of recent occupation. Footprints in dust and misplaced objects waited to provide more questions than answers. He drew back the heavy dark drapes rent with time by rot and their own weight. After pulling apart two French doors, he pushed ajar a pair of shutters and threw the dark, airless room open to a fresh summer's day. Light streamed in to illuminate rising ghostly clouds of dust. Turning to observe the room as light banished long resident shadows, he realized Elliott and Carrie were already searching.

Carrie descended on a pile of clothing heaped on an overstuffed and faded olive green, velvet wing chair. After sorting the garments, she held up two that appeared to be nursing uniforms of differing sizes, styles, and qualities.

She announced, "Again, there were two. There were two women, and they were both nurses."

Elliott reached out for the smaller one, a plain, faded and tattered garment. "This isn't a nursing uniform, but it is meant to look similar. This is for an assistant who prepares food, washes linens, changes beds, and empties bedpans. Assistants tend to wear clothing similar to nursing uniforms." As he held the drab garment up to examine the size, melancholy introspection entered his voice. "I probably stood next to this woman and never really noticed her."

Examining the second, larger garment, Elliott reported it to be a uniform worn by a student nurse. "An alumni of the School of Nursing would wear a different uniform with a cap, called a Flossie, and a pin."

Carrie took the garments back, inspecting their construction, turning out pockets.

Snow and Elliott spread out, searching. Ashes scattered on a side table next to an overstuffed wing chair caught Snow's attention. Stepping closer he found a small solid silver, curved box partly hidden by the seat cushion. Snow pocketed the cigar box.

Elliott reached under a dust encrusted chair, found a pin, and read, "Wise presiding over the decoction of medicine." A gold cross of St. George supported a circle with the serpent Hygiea entwined around a glass. Around the circle, the words *University of Maryland, Nurses Alumnae Assoc.* appeared in a border of red.

Elliott pronounced, "She was here. Only a member of the alumnae association would have this pin. It is a University of Maryland School Of Nursing pin designed by Tiffany's of New York, quite expensive." With the pin flat in his hand, he inviting them to inspect it.

Snow stepped over, held it, and scrutinized the pin as if it were a newly discovered species. A breeze, a whisper of change, sifted into the room.

Looking at the men standing with their backs to her, Carrie lifted something from the pile of discarded clothing. She slipped it under her apron into a deep side pocket of her skirt and picked up a glove without looking down. When she joined the men, Snow dropped the pin onto her hand.

"Life is different for young women today." Her remark, made through pursed lips, held a tone both wistful and touched with resentment. "More and more. I remember when the only trained nurses were the Daughters of Charity of St. Vincent de Paul in Emmitsburg. Thanks to them, Thomas Coode survived yellow fever in Cuba five years ago. Now..." Her voice trailed off as she rolled the pin in the palm of her hand.

Images of a red leaf, the first to change on the branch of a maple by the smokehouse, crossed Snow's mind. He gazed at the pin, considered changes sweeping through his world, and asked, "Are there any authentic nurse uniforms or nurse hats in the pile of clothing?"

Carrie returned the pin to Elliott and shook her head. "No, I only found those two. But I did find this one glove." She held out a left hand, white kidskin glove, wrist length with snaps labeled "made in France". It was stamped *Putt's Department Store, Imported.* Referred to as the 'glass palace' because of its display windows, Snow knew the Baltimore store, standing on the corner of Charles and Fayette Street, sold high-quality leather goods. It had been a favorite of Jane's, and he remembered his astonishment at the balance due on her account.

Carrie summarized. "We found two uniforms, a pin, and a left glove. There doesn't appear to be a right-hand glove, and I don't see a hat, a carpet bag, or a black medical bag."

They searched the corners of the room and behind drapes. They reexamined the uniforms, turned out pockets, checked seams, and felt along hems. Still, there was nothing confirming the identity of the woman buried on Sunday.

Reluctant to leave with so little, they stood in a circle gazing about the front parlor; Carrie clutching the glove, Elliott holding the pin firmly in his fist, and Snow lingering in his memories.

A voice called out from the woods.

Signaling the others to silence, Snow stepped softly out of the front parlor into the central hall. On his way toward the front door, he found a sheltered view of the Cawsin farmhouse front yard through a foyer window. Buddy Jenks stood half way across looking towards Carrie's little catboat tied at the dock. Snow relaxed and returned the pocket revolver to its bag. Then, he stepped into the yard and waved to Buddy.

"Hello, Judge. Thought you might be over here since the Rest was open. Put your ice blocks in that old icebox in the..." His voice halted when Elliott stepped out of the house to join Snow. Looking from Snow to Elliott and back again, Buddy relaxed when he spotted a bulge in the linen bag strung around Snow's shoulders. "Is Cousin Carry with you? Like to talk with her if I could."

Carrie stepped out and began walking across the yard. When Buddy shifted back and forth, looking at the ground, red-faced and obviously uncomfortable, Snow knew Sissy Jenks hadn't liked what she found at Darberry Farm. That gave him an idea.

Explaining the situation to Elliott, he told him more. "There are two Pinkerton Agents about to show up looking for you. Rolands will be with them." Elliott took a deep breath, pursing his lips. Snow continued, "If they did not know to search Darberry Farm, they would give up and sail back to Baltimore in a couple of days. James Miles mustn't know where you are. Sheriff Freeman is not likely to ask me. If the Pinkertons ask me where you are, I will say the last time I talked to you was today at Cawsin Farm which will be the truth."

Elliott smiled, looked sideways at him. Snow smiled back. "I heard all kinds of obfuscation for years while wearing black robes. But it would make things easier for Sheriff Freeman, for all of us, if the Pinkertons went on their way."

"Thank you, Judge." Elliott turned towards Snow, and a look of relief swept over him with the realization Snow was accepting his innocence.

After a pause to consider details, Elliott amended the plan. "I'll need to go back to Bluestone Farm. It might be best if I left James' horse there, took my medical bag, packed my belongings, and hiked over on foot. The presence of a horse at Darberry Farm would give me away. I'll tell Miles I am going back to Baltimore. The Sheriff and the Pinkertons might think I left on the *Northumberland* if I was seen walking in the direction of Broome's Wharf. Would you please ask Mrs. Darberry to pack a basket of food for me? Could you sail over to Darberry Farm and tell me when the Pinkertons are gone? Nothing needing to be cooked, so I won't have to lite a fire. If I ask the Miles for food, they will know I am still in the area."

"Yes. That would work." Impressed with how rapidly Elliott worked out those details, Snow was convinced Elliott agreed with the plan. Their conversation ended as Carrie and Buddy approached. Snow was surprised to see Carrie smiling, not showing disappointment.

Hat off, turning the brim around in his hands, Buddy stood tongue-tied until a nod of assurance from Carrie prompted him to begin.

"Your honor," he began. Snow smiled knowing people wanted something when they addressed him using his title. "Mrs. Darberry tells me that you might be looking for a caretaker at the Rest, for when you go back to Baltimore for the winter. Would you let me, my Sissy, and our little ones live at the Rest this winter? We would take real good care of it."

Snow bowed his head in thought and observed the young man's hopeful expression begin to fade. "I think we could discuss it and maybe come to terms." Buddy brightened, grinning broadly.

Snow gave Carrie his arm and turned to Elliott. "Have a safe journey." Elliott nodded and walked toward the horse, still tethered in the woods.

To Carrie, he said, "I will come back for your little craft tomorrow as you won't be needing it today. Do you need those baskets?"

She changed the plan with, "Why don't you sail it back down the Run for me now? I can walk back through the woods with Buddy. At this point, we missed our lunch. So, I need to start dinner early.

Ready to demonstrate his usefulness, Buddy interrupted with, "Your block ice was my last delivery. I could scull the boat back down to the Rest, and you could walk Mrs. Darberry through the woods. It won't take me long. Tide ebbed an hour ago. On its way in now." Carrie agreed.

Snow nodded. "Yes. Thank you. That would be very convenient."

After watching Buddy pick his way down the crumbling dock to the boat, Snow returned to close up the front parlor. With the key in hand, he stood before the door and wondered why he should bother locking it. All the years these doors and windows were locked and shuttered, hiding Jane's grief, gave him insight into his dead wife's state of mind. Snow glanced around the room and detected something blue against a wall under a chair. Heart beating in anticipation, he took four long strides and lifted it. The lined jacket, faded beyond his memory, rose before him. Hattie's mourning brooch of Annabelle Cawsin Wells had left its mark where it was pinned in the weave of the lapel.

Through the open French windows and out to the Run, he watched Buddy scull away from the dock. He looked past the unlocked front parlor door, back down the central hall, through the broken double doors into the back yard. Carrie was on her way along the path in the woods. Dropping the jacket, Snow left the house heading for the path. The key lay abandoned in the lock of the opened door.

Snow was almost to the path when a single shot echoed through the trees. In two running strides, he had the Pocket Pistol in hand before reason prevailed. Crouched, he entered the woods and worked his way around trees parallel to the path until he had a view down to the first bend. Looking left to right and back again, he took in every movement, anything seeming out of place. All was still and silent. Abruptly, Blue Jays, at first hushed by the shot, shrieked and darted through the high canopy. Two large crows, with wing spans a yard wide, glided up the path, their "koww, koww" filling the woods with alarm. A slight movement on Snow's part sent them diving, wings folded, into trees on the other side. With gun double-handed, he reached the stream and forded it in one leap. Stooping lower for several strides, he continued through underbrush. Fear for Carrie, thoughts of her felled by that shot, propelled him toward the Rest.

Using the Rest's summer kitchen for cover, he emerged from trees and reconnoitered the yard and gardens. Carrie stood on the back porch steps facing him with the missing Remington 95 double-barreled derringer gripped in her right hand and a good size, semi-headless cottontail rabbit dangling upside down from her left.

Both relief and anger swept through him as he swung around and leaned against the summer kitchen's back wall, bending over, catching his breath. He heard Carrie cross the yard, and hesitate out of sight. "William, are you alright? You sounded like a bear thrashing through the woods."

Snow stepped out from behind the shed, Pocket Police held down by his side, and looked hard at Carrie and then at the derringer.

Contrition crossed Carrie's face. "Oh, William, you were frightened for me. I'm sorry. When I came around the bend in the woods, this cottontail was sitting there so still in the middle of the path. Before I gave it a thought, I had shot the thing. Almost took off the head. This derringer, small as it is, packs quite a kick. I should have called back to you, told you what I did. I'm so sorry."

Snow returned his pistol back to the bag and reached out for the derringer. Silently with hesitation and a defiant expression, Carrie gave it to him. After placing it with the pistol, he rubbed his left arm, and coughed.

Carrie declared, "I did pay some attention to your warning about going about alone." When Snow still didn't respond to her excuse, she took a better look at him. "I'll make you some tea. You should rest a little."

Snow thought, "I'd rather drink three fingers of Jenk's Best.", but said, "Give me the rabbit, and I'll dress it for you." Reluctantly, she handed over her prize.

After removing what remained of the head with a quick cut of the summer kitchen boning knife, Snow removed the feet. He pulled the velvet soft pelt loose along haunches, torso, and back, before peeling it off like a jacket to reveal the sweet tender meat. Making a shallow slice down the abdomen and through the breastbone, he lifted the rabbit and removed the organs intact by inserting two fingers into the cavity. He hung the rabbit to bleed out, scrubbed his arms to the elbows with water and lye soap, and went down the hill to begin evening chores.

By then, Buddy had sculled the catboat back down the Run, and tied up. Mud caked his overalls from the several times he pulled it out of muddy shallows along the way. Stopping at the barn, Buddy asked about the shot, but Snow only said they had rabbit for dinner. He was relieved when Buddy said he would have to hurry along, and went up the hill to his mules and wagon.

By the time Snow finished the evening feeding, lugged water buckets, milked the cow, and finally collected those eggs, Carrie had washed the rabbit. Leaving it whole, she rubbed it with salt pork, pepper, nutmeg, and mace before spitting it for roasting over an open fire. When he arrived with the milk and eggs, she brought the rabbit out to him along with a tin mug of tea.

Standing by the back yard fire pit, Snow waited for his fire to burn down to embers for roasting without scorching, and examined the cigar cutter he found in the Cawsin farm kitchen house. It was double ended with two steel mechanisms. One end cut a triangular slot of about a half inch and the other a flat cut slot about a quarter inch. The scene on the sterling silver handle was a C.S.A. soldier on horseback waving the flag of the Confederate States of America. One monogram of initials, possibly F. R., were scratched out and replaced with J. F. S. He placed it back in his pocket.

Tending fire and sipping a second mug of Carrie's tea, Snow was surprised to hear Jenks' mules and wagon creaking down Snow's Rest Road once more.

Buddy called out from his wagon seat, "On my way home. Thought to bring your mail and papers from St. Mary's Post Office. Mrs. Abell let me take them. I told her I was your new caretaker. Nice size rabbit you shot."

When Snow answered that Mrs. Darberry shot the rabbit, it was Buddy's turn to be surprised. It occurred to Snow Jenks had other reasons for coming all the way to the Rest again when Buddy jumped down from the wagon and brought him the mail. Snow thanked him and waited while Buddy stood shifting back and forth.

Finally, Snow took a guess and began the conversation with, "So, tell me about Dr. Elliott."

"Well, he's coming down Broome's Wharf Road with his bags. He offers me a quarter to take him to the dock. When we get there, he boards the *Northumberland* just before she casts off for Baltimore."

Snow gazed into his fire and gathered his thoughts. Buddy glanced at Snow for a reaction to this news before continuing. "That new first mate, Thomas Coode, the one Carrie raised, he took a special interest in Elliott. Came down the dock. Hailed me. Asked a lot of questions."

Snow thought Ben Elliott might have a good chance of arrest on arriving in Baltimore with that nurse's pin in his possession. But, he said, "I don't think Thomas Coode and Ben Elliott ever met. Thomas probably wondered about the medical bag."

"Think it was more than that." Buddy's response had the tone of a question he was hesitant to ask. Taking three cigars from his overall bib pocket, he bit the ends off two with his teeth and lit them in the fire. He handed one lit and the one still banded to Snow.

Staring at the train engine and the words 'Moore's Imported Turkish' on the band, Snow hesitated controlling his expression before looking up.

"Thoughtful of you, Buddy." He saw no evidence of guile in Buddy's open smile. "These are different. I haven't seen them before. Do the Broome's carry them at the store?"

"No, no. Josiah and I, we get them free from that buyer. Comes down and looks over our tobacco real early when we start cutting. Deals exclusive. Josiah and I built this special long drying barn. Our crop gets more air, dries better. Buyer comes back and watches us pack his strips. That 'Imported Turkish' is a joke. It's imported all the way from St. Mary's County."

Snow forced a smile. "What buyer is that?"

"The one I was telling you I saw the day that nurse arrived. Didn't talk to him that day. He must have talked to the Milburns over in Ridge and then gone on up Leonardtown later in the week. Josiah and I, we was worried for a while. Worried he was after another supply here or up county. But he came back to us and talked to Josiah this week."

In silence, Snow and Buddy drew several times until the sweet, spicy smoke filled their mouth and trailed out their nostrils. Snow blew a ring of smoke and asked, "So, what did this buyer say for himself?"

"Just said he'd be back for our hogsheads. Said he trusted us. Didn't want to take a look inside."

"This buyer came all the way down here from Baltimore to tell you that?"

Buddy took his time blowing an even bigger ring than Snow's. "Maybe not. He was comin' from Leonardtown. Might want to see we don't sell to someone else. Might be thinking of sticking us with a lower price later. If we wait for him." Buddy drew on his cigar and let the smoke drift out. "Elliott was gettin' on board. Buyer couldn't take his eyes off him. Just said I didn't know much. Buyer hung around watching and listening with his back to me. Got right back on board the *Northumberland* when Coode was finished talking."

"What's his name, the buyer?"

"Says his name is Albert M. Sparks Jr. Says he's great nephew to the owner of Moore's Tobacco. Brags he'll be owner when the old man dies. Throws money around like he already owns the company. Even in summer, he dresses in a jacket with pleats like the bottom of a woman's dress. Sweats up a storm and has to carry it over his arm. And one of those wide brim hats with a crease down the crown like someone hit it with a bat. Don't know how he keeps it on his head when the wind comes up. Eye for the ladies. Got himself in trouble over Piney Point a few years ago. Likes to gamble, too. Owes a quite a bit here and there. But, he knows good tobacco. We always hear from him, but we never let him buy on letters of credit. Cash up front only."

"Well, it's getting late. Thank you for bringing the mail and for the smokes. Stop by tomorrow. We'll walk the Rest and get an agreement worked out." Buddy perked up, nodded, and took his leave. While he watched Jenks' mules and wagon disappear down Snow's Rest Road, Snow wondered if Elliott would disappear on his way to Baltimore.

Hearing the screen door slap shut behind him, Snow swallowed the rest of his tea and placed the spitted rabbit over the ready fire.

"I was stirring up pan biscuits and chopping sweet potatoes when Buddy came by again. Did you two work out an agreement?"

Snow pondered telling Carrie that Elliott had sailed for Baltimore, but decided to take up on her chosen topic instead. "Buddy brought the mail as he considers himself our caretaker now."

Carrie raised an eyebrow at his use of the word 'our'. She stepped toward the fire with the covered iron pot of vegetables, dumpling dough, and lard. Visions of the unknown victim's burnt hand and clothing flashed into Snow's mind as he reached for the pot. "I'll do that. It would be better if you kept your distance from the flames."

"Don't put that on the flames. It should be to the side on hot stones and turned every few minutes."

Snow smiled at Carrie's commanding tone. "This takes me back to cooking in camp during the War. This would have been a feast."

"Well, maybe you know what you're doing." She conceded. Reading his thoughts, she added, "Do you think he held her hand in the fire to make her tell him?"

He looked into her eyes, read the horror she felt. "It is possible. It might also be possible that she was trying to retrieve something from the flames, like a letter he threw in to destroy. You are thinking it was a man?"

Carrie nodded, trapped in the terror of possibilities, unable to put it to words. Snow put these thoughts to words for them both. "Hattie isn't strong enough. Also, she has no motive."

Carrie speculated. "But she might be a witness. Might have stolen the clothes, the carpet bag, and the medical bag. By now, she might be far off somewhere pretending to be a trained nurse. She did train with Dr. Radcliff on Solomons Island. What would have been *his* reason?"

"We'll know his reason better when we know who he is." Handing her the cigar band and cutter found in the Cawsin farm kitchen house, he added, "He may have left these behind. I took them to show

Freeman. Considering all the times I was over to Cawsin Farm, I don't know how I didn't see these before."

After examining them, she handed them back and commented that we don't see what we are not looking for. After a few moments, he took out the unlit cigar Buddy had given him, and she asked, "Did you find this one there?"

He shook his head. "No. Buddy gave it to me just now."

Surprise in her expression was quickly replaced with denial. "Buddy would never have done such a horrible thing. I've known him all his life, held him as a baby. Buddy Jenks is a good man."

"I'm not accusing him of anything. Buddy got this cigar from a tobacco buyer who is related to the owner of Moore's Tobacco. It was the same buyer he saw the day the nurse arrive."

"And where is this buyer now?"

"Buddy says he left on the *Northumberland* for Baltimore this afternoon." Snow decided not to tell her that Elliott was also on the *Northumberland*, at least not for now.

"What are you going to do?"

"I'll show these to Freeman when he comes down with the Pinkertons. We'll decide later who else to tell." She nodded. Snow turned the black iron pan around against the fire and the rabbit on the spit. "It's been a long and difficult day. I could use three fingers of whiskey, and would be honored if you join me with a glass of sherry."

She smiled, went to do his bidding, brought back a half glass of sherry for herself, and two fingers of rye for Snow. He smiled when she claimed her fingers were smaller. Sitting beside the smoking fire on a two-foot wide split oak log, they ate camp style, tearing pieces of rabbit from the spit to eat in hand while using forks to eat sweet potatoes and dumpling directly from the pan. At the end of the meal with the fire gone out, they washed away the grease and set the black iron pan to soak.

Snow invited Carrie to join him on the front porch and offered her another glass of sherry when he refilled his whiskey. To his surprise, she consented and even sat next to him on the wicker divan.

Silence settled over them with weariness of the day. Sun set across the river and dipped slowly behind the trees until one last ray reached out to sparkle on the river. A gold and silver lock had fallen from her loosening swept up hair, curling loose and silken down her shoulder. He reached out, fingered it fondly. She looked up, a wryness in her crooked smile.

Leaning towards her, searching her eyes, he recited from Shelley.

'And the sunlight clasps the earth,
And the moonbeams kiss the sea;--
What are all these kissings worth,
If thou kiss not me?'

She threw back her head and laughed. "And how often have you used those lines to get a kiss, William Snow?"

"Only once. ...tonight." He realized it as their first laugh together, while he pulled her to him for their first kiss.

A breeze slipped from the river up the hill and into the Rest. Somewhere within the old manor house, Snow heard hinges slowly creaking the sound of an opening door.

Chapter 10: The Chiming Clock

Down Time's quaint stream,
Without an oar
We are enforced to sail
Our Port a secret
　　Emily Dickinson (1830 -1886)

In the morning, a premonition of autumn breezed its way into the Rest blowing one solitary, scarlet leaf through the central hall. When the chiming mantle clock struck seven loudly in cooler air, the sun was barely up a half hour. Snow closed windows, shut doors, and made the coffee. After adding cooled milk from a pitcher kept in the icebox, he put Carrie's mug on the stove skirt within her reach and brushed against her arm. The ends of a shawl wrapped around her shoulders swept the stove top as she reached for her mug. Standing behind her, he pulled the shawl ends under her arms and tied them behind her back. She smiled but didn't glance up.

Stewed tomatoes and bacon bubbled in a black iron frying pan on the summer kitchen stove. Carrie cracked and broke four eggs onto a plate and slipped their sunny faces into bacon fat sizzling in another pan. She spooned hot fat over the eggs rather than turn the fresh yokes that break easily and run. Edges of egg whites browned into a lacy crisp around the four eggs sunny side up. Snow placed two hot biscuits on each plate, spooned stewed tomatoes over them, topped them with bacon strips, and held them out as Carrie added the eggs. Lastly, she placed lids on the pans to keep out flies and moved them to the side warming shelf while they ate.

With coffee mugs and plates, they retreated to the back porch. A silence of contentment settled over them as they ate side by side. A few red and yellow leaves tumble across the yard. Their shoulders brushed as she took his mug and then walked across to the summer kitchen to pour from the percolator warming on the side shelf. Along with the mugs, she took the iron pan of stewed tomatoes and walked back toward the porch. Seeing Carrie's hands full, Snow held the screened door open and caught it on a hook. He took the mugs to the table before retrieving the tin pitcher of milk from the icebox.

She sat next to him and said, "When were you going to tell me Ben Elliott sailed for Baltimore on the *Northumberland* yesterday?"

He smiled at her sidewise, "Thought you would figure it out."

"Well, Ben wanted a food basket. Buddy came by, and you two were all secretive. You never asked me to pack the basket. So, Ben changed his plans."

Recalling Carrie was across the Cawsin Farm back yard when Elliott asked for a cache of food, Snow commented, "Well, your hearing is excellent." Then he told her the rest of the story about the buyer and shared his concerns that Elliott faced possible arrest for the disappearance or murder of Dorothea Snareborn.

Continuing to eat, Carrie reflected on this news and measured her response. "Yesterday, in the Cawsin farmhouse front parlor, did you see the nurse pin before Ben picked it off the floor?"

Snow shook his head, and she continued. "I like Ben Elliott, but I must say we don't know for sure the pin was on the floor under that chair. What if it came out of his pocket?" She paused to watch Snow's reaction. "Am I too suspicious?"

"Maybe you are, but you are making a point. Ben is likable, but he is also an inept liar. He seemed genuinely surprised to find it. What reason would he have to lie?"

When she shrugged her shoulders, he shared his thoughts. "There are questions about this buyer. Sparks appears at every turn. We don't know very much about him. Why was he interested in Ben Elliott? Buddy Jenks doesn't trust him even though the Jenks have done business with him for some time."

Carrie stared across the yard toward the path in the woods. "There are two more important questions. Who is the young woman we buried on Monday? Where is Dorothea Snareborn? I might know the answer to the first question."

Pausing a forkful of smothered biscuit in midair, Snow turned to face her, his mouth still open. She took a deep breath before beginning. "Yesterday, I saw something I wanted, something I needed, a book among the clothes in the front parlor. It was a copy of <u>Notes On Nursing: What It Is, And What It Is Not</u>, by Florence Nightingale. If Dr. Miles asks me to be a traveling nurse, this book will be valuable to me. This morning when I finally opened it...well there's an inscription on the inside cover and a photograph tucked in the back." She reached under her apron, took it from her skirt pocket, and placed it between them. The photograph slipped out.

NOTES
ON
NURSING
By
FLORENCE NIGHTINGALE

Snow opened the cover and read,

"To Dorothea Snareborn, R.N., Congratulations. Your cap and pin are well deserved.
Yours truly,
Mrs. Katherine A. Taylor, Superintendent of Nurses."

In the photograph, several women in nursing uniforms with ankle length hemlines stood at the foot of beds in a hospital ward. Some of the women wore uniforms consisting of white caps, full aprons, collars, and sleeve guards over dark colored dresses. Some wore half aprons and collars, but no hats or sleeve guards. Several women in dark dresses and aprons held bed linens and stood behind the uniformed nurses. One senior nurse wearing a more elaborate cap sat keeping records at a desk with a telephone. Carrie turned the photograph over.

Written on the back, he read,

'With best wishes to Mary, May we both escape to a better life. Fondly, Dorothea'

"So, now we know who she was. Or, maybe we do. If Ben Elliott is telling the truth, she is not Dot Snareborn. She may be this Mary. Possibly she was a training nurse or a housekeeper. Do you think Miss Snareborn is still alive and perhaps in hiding?"

Carrie nodded and turned the photograph back over to point at a group of nurses in various uniforms standing at the foot of patient beds. One shorter, younger woman in a dark dress held a towel and stood between them. Carrie pointed to one of the nurses and then to the assistant. "These two might be mistaken for sisters. They appear alike except one is taller. If Ben was here, he would tell us if the taller one is his Dot."

"Or the fiancé, Rolands, can tell us if Sheriff Freeman brings him down here. He knows Rolands and two Pinkerton agents are coming by steamboat from Baltimore to Leonardtown looking for Dr. Elliott. Freeman may use the developed film for identification." Snow knew Freeman would enjoy showing off the photographs and frustrating the Pinkerton Agents.

He speculated, "They may not come here at all." He saw Carrie's skeptical look. "But they probably will. If they are on the *Calvert,* she went up river early this morning without stopping at Broome's Wharf. She'll dock at Grayson's Wharf, cross to Virginia, come back to Piney Point, and then up to Leonardtown and Bushwood. The agents will disembark in Leonardtown looking for Freeman. They may be here by Friday, or Freeman might sail them down himself to keep track of them. When they don't find Elliott, he'll put them back on the *Northumberland* when she goes back up the *Bay* on Thursday afternoon. The sooner he can send them on their way the better."

Carrie reached out for the book, putting her hand over Snow's. "I could make excellent use of this when I go on home visits. Dr. Miles will need me more now that Dr. Elliott is gone. One way or another, I can't see Ben coming back." Snow heard a slight quiver in her voice, thought her hand trembled as it touched his.

"We'll need to show these to Freeman. It is proof of a connection between the two women. The inscription on the photograph makes it possible they were both running away. The questions are from whom and why. If Freeman, or the Pinkertons insist on keeping this book, I promise to buy you another."

Carrie's hand slipped away. As she sat straighter, her expression stiffened.

"Well, I will be holding you to your promise, Judge Snow."

An oak leaf, yellow and speckled brown, drifted in lazy circles across the yard. Caught in a rush of breeze, it lifted through the open screen door landing against the rim of Snow's dish. Whispers of change stirring through Cawsin Farm front parlor came to his mind. He remembered the turning leaf.

When Snow glanced at her, Carrie had turned away smoothing her apron. He cleared his throat. "If you've decided... I don't mean to pry, but I was wondering if you have an agreement with Dr. Miles."

Hands folded in her lap, Carrie took a deep breath. "Flora Miles and I have discussed details of an arrangement. On days James has office calls at the Great Mills house, I will act as a receptionist; organizing patients, keeping records of diagnosis and treatments, recording payments. On days James makes house calls, I will accompany him and keep the same records. There will be other days when I follow up on his house calls as a community nurse. Flora has started sewing two uniforms for me from gabardine cloth Thomas brought. James arranged the purchase of a pony and cart. Broomes Wharf store has three I can try out, and James will buy whichever one I like. His Morgan gelding is too spirited for me to handle. When I am not nursing, I will earn my room and board sewing and mending for Flora and James. Of course, I would have to live at Bluestone Farm."

Snow retorted, "And what will you do in your leisure time?" This met pressed lips and a sharp look.

Carrie retorted, "The Miles have every intention of paying me for my services in addition to allowing me to live with them in their lovely home. James is soft hearted and some patients take advantage. The Miles family is of a mind that I will more than make up for my wages by insisting on payment from patients who are perfectly able to pay."

Snow blushed slightly and nodded. "I apologize. My remark was uncalled for." While he finished eating, he reflected on all the weeks Carrie had taken care of him without compensation. "You have been kind to me, Carrie. I can only imagine what a state I would be in now if you hadn't sailed over here that morning with your basket of food. I have grown quite fond of you and was hoping you might consider helping me reorganize the Rest for the winter." He hesitated. "...and coming up to Baltimore." Her eyes widen and a smile lift her features. He continued, "I will be at a loss without you. Jane never actually had a housekeeper, only maids and cooks. She preferred to supervise everything herself." He watched Carrie's face stiffen, the smile fade. Her expression changed to match the chill of early autumn.

From her lap, she held out a small silk pouch and opened it to spill out two similar rings. Examining the rings, he realized with a start that one was from the hand of Mary. Freeman had passed it to Carrie for examination when they were attempting to identify the body in the Run.

Carrie anticipated Snow's next comment. "He never asked for it back. So, I think the Pinkertons and fiancé will definitely be coming to see you."

"And you." He thought. Staring at the other ring, more elaborate than the first, he asked, "And this one?"

"As you know, I raised Thomas Coode and his sister, Ellen Mae, after their grandmother died. The poor little things lost their parents and grandmother three years apart. Your Jane sailed down from Baltimore especially to ask me for help. I have to admit I was at a desperate point in my life. As years passed, Old Benjamin became increasingly dependent on me to manage the boat yard finances as well as keep house and raise his grandchildren. He never paid well, but he provided for all our needs and paid for Richard's education. At one point, I told Benjamin I was considering a move back to my farm. He asked me to marry him and gave me this engagement ring. Months passed, and he continually delayed setting a wedding date. Later, I discovered this ring had belonged to his late wife, Eleanor. When Ben asked why I took it off, I said I would put it back on when he set a date. Neither of us ever did." Snow picked this second ring from her hand, examining the stones.

She explained, "It's a 'dearest ring'. The stones are diamond, emerald, amethyst, ruby, emerald, sapphire, and topaz. But, you only give it to one woman, one time." He nodded and placed it back in her open hand, comprehending the depths of his mistake, pausing on the cusp of a decision.

Sounds of wagon wheels creaked along Snow's Farm Road. Carrie stood, cleared off her plate, and was standing at the house kitchen door by the time Buddy and Josiah Jenks came into view; Buddy with his wagon and Josiah behind him on horseback. Two laborers sat on straw in the back of Buddy's wagon dangling their legs over the tailgate. Buddy sat facing backwards toward the others, one common rein slack in his hand. All four men were laughing at some remark. The businesslike mules clopped to their usual spot in the shade by the water trough.

Laughter faded as Buddy and Josiah dismounted. The laborers jumped off and stood behind the wagon almost out of sight, their dark faces peering over the sideboards. Hats in hand, Buddy and Josiah crossed the yard, mounted the back porch steps, and waited to be invited in.

Snow greeted them and invited them in for coffee which the brothers declined.

Placing the paper on the table, Buddy announced, "Judge Snow, I have your *Sun*, but there isn't any mail. Is it too early in the morning to do business? I could start my ice deliveries and come back later."

Snow picked up the paper. "No, Buddy, we can walk the Rest now. I'm finished with my breakfast."

Turning to Carrie, he thanked her for his meal. Then he quickly scrutinized headlines on the front page of *The Sun*. These included the report of a second game 6 to 0 win by the Pittsburgh Pirates over the Philadelphia Phillies, which clinched the National League Championship for the Pirates. Below was an article about a playoff to be called the World Series and played in early October between the Pittsburg Pirates and the Boston Americans. Odds makers were giving the edge to Boston and a pitcher named Young whom Boston raided from St. Louis for the phenomenal sum of $3,500. Snow lost interest in baseball when the bankrupted Baltimore Orioles had moved to New York and became the Yankees. He expected they would fade into obscurity just as the fate of Dorothea Snareborn had faded from front page coverage.

From the screened porch, he led Josiah and Buddy down the hill toward the barns. Buddy waved his hat toward his wagon, and his hired men followed at a distance. "Judge Snow, I brought my men, Travis and Adrian Harris, so they could see what needs to be done. If there is anything you want them to do, just tell me."

Snow looked back at the two men and nodded. "Well, I haven't done the morning chores yet."

"We'll get right on that." Buddy walked back and spoke to the Harris brothers. After glancing at Snow in surprise, they separated from the group and headed toward the barn.

Josiah grinned. "I think they are a little surprised you do your own milking, Judge."

Snow smiled. "I was raised in the country, Josiah. It doesn't go away."

Boundaries and corners of Rest land were clearly marked. Ancient beginning trees that stood on these corners two hundred years earlier had long since fallen. Other markers took their place. Piles of stones and stone slabs with chiseled dates established corners. Snow's Run set the northwest boundary.

Buddy remarked a caretaker's house was needed. Snow agreed Buddy and his family could live in part of the Rest this winter and build in the spring if all went well. Upkeep and repairs were needed this year. The Jenks would handle sale of current crops to cover this year's taxes. Next year they would make a new agreement. Josiah pointed out that corn, tobacco, and hay were poor as the year was dry. Snow pointed out that John Lundy put up enough first cutting hay for animals at the Rest. The sow should be bred and three of this year's female shoats kept to increase hog production. The rest could be butchered before Christmas. Snow wanted two corned hams and 50 pounds of sausage sent to Baltimore. The Jenks family could have what was left to eat or sell for tax money. This season his cow calved a bull. It could be slaughtered for grass fed veal as it was less than 20 weeks. Snow wanted 30 pounds top of the round corned veal and the rest was Buddy's. If they wanted milk, the cow must be bred again. Buddy knew a quiet bull that usually threw heifers. Snow said Cawsin Farm could be used as a wood lot as long as wood was taken from what had been fields at one time. Snow hoped they would clear these and make them productive again. Property taxes had climbed to 16 cents on $100. The Jenks should be able to make the taxes from sale of tobacco, corn, hogs, and wood. Josiah pointed out the tax on whiskey had been over a dollar a gallon for the last eight years. Although Snow didn't express his misgivings about their compliance with tax laws, he was adamant the Jenks could not operate a distillery on his property. Josiah said that was not a problem as they had other arrangements. And so the negotiations went on throughout the morning. By the time they returned to the Rest, the morning chores were done, and the barns were mucked out. Adrian's wife, Phyllis, had arrived to cook and clean under Carrie's direction.

Through the afternoon, Carrie helped Snow plan arrangement of the furniture. Travis and Adrian came in the cool evening to complete the plan. Snow wrote a list of his personal items and books for shipment to Baltimore. Other items, among them Jane's china, books, the typewriter, would be packed and stored in the attic. Some front parlor furniture would go up to the sewing room making room for the piano and dining room furniture in the front parlor. The growing young Jenks family would be delighted with the back bedroom, house kitchen, pantry, dining room, and Jane's sitting room. Carrie's efficiency told him she had planned this arrangement some time back. Snow leaned against the piano, fingered the two old quilts covering it, and said he would 'sleep on it'.

Change bustled about the Rest ignoring his reticence. Overwhelmed with the pace of it, he went out to his front porch, sat himself down, stared down the fields, out the Run, and across the river. His chest felt tight and his arms heavy. Carrie brought him tea, warm buttered bread, sliced late peaches dripping with juice, and left him to his solitude. He finished the light supper and retrieved three fingers of Jenks Best along with his nightly smoke. The bottle came back to the porch with him. Later, seated on the wicker setae part way through the whiskey, he reached into his pocket for a box of matches, and retrieved the silver cigar box instead. Flipping it open, he discovered a hole-punched steamboat ticket folded above two Van Bibber Little Cigars. Behind him, the mantle clock chimed the changing of time as light dimmed to early dusk. Needing companionship, he ambled up the creaking center hall stairs to his library in search of an understanding title and read himself to sleep.

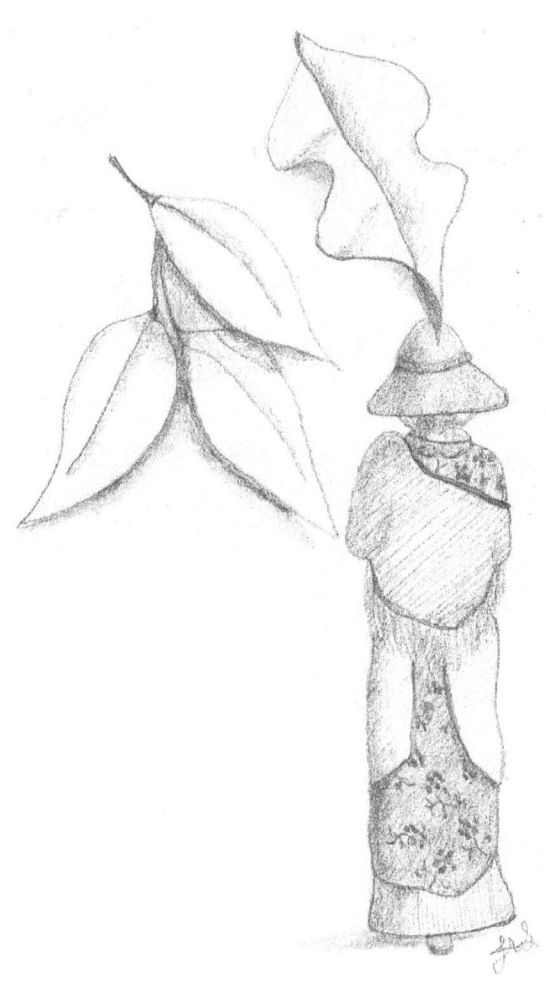

Chapter 11: The Glance Back

From one stage of our being to the next
We pass unconscious o'er a slender bridge,
The momentary work of unseen hands,
Which crumbles down behind us; looking back,
And, marvelling how we won
To where we stand,
Content ourselves to call the builder Chance.
 James Russell Lowell (1819 - 1891)

Scent of pine needles drifted into his sleep. He lay on his stomach, head on his left hand, obscured in a clump of mountain laurel. Before him in shifting haze, a grey-clad rider sat poised on a dark horse. The rider's hand, firm and flat against the mount's neck, demanded the war horse stand rigid and silent. Snow grasped something solid, the action of a rifle. The horse and gray figure stood motionless, a statue in repose on a granite outcrop. Before them, a savage, thousand foot descent opened against a backdrop of massive peaks rising into mist across a cavernous valley. Turning its Grecian head toward Snow, the statue became David. Brother David stared into Snow's face, into his eyes, into his soul. William Snow raised the .44 caliber Henry repeater and aimed into fog drifting across the distance between them. He scanned the panorama and glanced back again. The gray-clad rider and mount transformed into a man wearing a Weems Line uniform. As he tossed in the sheets of his solitary slumber, Snow gripped the rifle to discover instead his volume of Ambrose Bierce's <u>Tales of Soldiers and Civilians</u> laying open on the bed. Recovery from his rapid, erratic heartbeat was protracted. He returned the book to his library where he found the bottle of Jenks Best now only a third full.

Later, washed and shaved, Snow gradually descended the creaking central hall stairs. As he entered the dining room,

Adrian Harris' wife, Phyllis, appeared wordlessly from the kitchen hall holding a sizeable tray and placed it on the sideboard where a coffee pot kept hot under a cozy. On the dining room table, in the midst of eight empty chairs, one plate of Jane's best country china waited. Sitting before the solitary place setting, Snow unfolded the napkin across his lap. After pouring his coffee, Phyllis served him a breakfast of poached pears, ham omelet, beef hash, warmed potatoes, and cornbread. He thanked her. She nodded, moved the coffee pot to the table, and left for the kitchen. Empty chairs stared at him, chairs his father, mother, brother, and wife once occupied. The room expanded with each hollow tick of the clock or penetrating clink of fork and knife.

Sounds echoed through the Rest from the back yard; the crash of boards unloaded from a wagon, the grating sing of a two man, crosscut saw, the rhythm of hammers. He stood and threw his napkin down, angered that he was not consulted.

She walked into the room. In a straw bonnet tied with a pink scarf, her pink flowered chintz dress, and white Sunday gloves, Carrie appeared fresh and lovely.

He smiled. "Will you be joining me?"

She opened her mouth to speak, and closed it again. After a moment, she replied, "No thank you. I have eaten. Buddy is here with the Harris brothers to begin work on the cabin. The Harris family needs somewhere to live while completing the repairs you requested. As you were still abed, I told them to start. Buddy is taking me to Broome's Wharf to pick out a cart and pony before beginning his ice deliveries. When I get back, we can continue rearranging the Rest. Buddy and Sissy will move in on Monday. Just in case Sheriff Freeman and the Pinkertons arrive before my return, I will leave that ring with you." Saying this, she placed the small silk pouch on the table between them.

They stood looking at each other, searching each other's eyes, but the moment passed. Snow nodded. "Well, take your time." She bustled out down the kitchen hall along her new path in life.

Ringed by empty chairs, he refilled his coffee, lifted his plate, and walked out to his front porch to keep the river and fields company. Down at the barn, one of the Harris brothers let the cow out to pasture after milking. Melancholy for the loss of his country life settled over Snow followed by an impulse to be gone.

Out on the river, a cat boat sailed into view on a reach, fell off into the Run, and dropped sail approaching the dock. Finishing the last mouthful of breakfast, Snow watched it and sipped coffee. The boat's sole occupant tied up and stepped up to the dock. Still in his first mate's uniform and cap, Thomas Coode leisurely worked his way up the hill towards the Rest. A limp from his war experience in Cuba bothered him today. Snow observed Thomas' walking stick, one not brought on his previous visit. A short way up, he began occasional use of the cane to relieve his limp and speed his progress.

As Thomas drew closer, the nature of the long, narrow, dark weapon became clear. It had a small handle, a ball completely swallowed by Thomas' grip. Snow recognized the Baritsu walking stick. Shortly after publication of Arthur Conan Doyle's <u>The Adventure of the Empty House</u>, Ira Fader brought a Baritsu to Snow's after dinner smoking session. The gentlemen smokers played with it, lunging and releasing its deadly, hidden steel stiletto. So, Thomas had a new toy but for what purpose?

Snow rose and went in to retrieve the silver cigar box along with his derringer. After securing the cigar box in his pocket, he concealed the derringer behind a spittoon under his wicker setae. By the time Coode reached the front garden, Phyllis had slipped into the porch with a fresh pot of coffee and a plate of cornbread.

Snow walked to the porch screen door, held it open, and waved. "Thomas, what a pleasant surprise. To what do we owe this pleasure? I'm just finishing breakfast. Would you like something to eat, some cornbread perhaps?"

Thomas raised his hand, not so much in greeting, but in answer to Snow's question. His hand held a large envelope. "Thank you, Judge. Coffee and cornbread would be appreciated. I have a document for you."

On the steps, Thomas tucked the cane under his arm, and they shook hands. Handing over the envelope, he dropped wearily into a wicker chair, stretching his leg out before him. Phyllis appeared with plates and utensils for the cornbread and poured the coffee. While Thomas stirred in cream and sugar, Snow took a furtive glance at the envelope. The office seal of Warfield and Snow was not damaged. He placed the letter aside.

"I'll look at this later. Thomas, you go ahead and eat. Then you can tell me how you came to bring this."

Not standing on courtesy, Thomas talked between mouthfuls of coffee and cornbread. "Last night,... just before *Northumberland* cast off,... a law clerk from Warfield and Snow,... came down the Light Street Pier." Thomas paused his tale to wash down another mouthful of cornbread, and Snow replenished Thomas' cup and plate. After eating the last mouthful, Thomas continued his explanation. "Asked me to deliver that envelope to you. Apparently, you offered him a bonus if he got the answer to you by today. He missed yesterday's afternoon mail, so it wouldn't get here until *Potomac* came through on Monday. The clerk considered taking passage to bring it personally. He recognized me from when I attended Aunt Jane's funeral. So, I offered to take it for him..." Smiling, Thomas added "...and split the bonus. Captain Geoghegan gave me leave to visit you. I'll reboard the *Northumberland* when she comes back this afternoon. She'll cross back from Virginia to Piney Point and come up St. Mary's River for a call at Porto Bello. Then she'll cross over to Broome's Wharf before heading back up to Baltimore." While he ate and talked, Thomas looked back and forth between Snow and the envelope.

Snow sipped coffee feigning little interest in the envelope. "Thank you for going out of your way to deliver this document. I will thank Bill Geoghegan for giving you leave when next I see him." Snow reached into his pocket fingering the silver box, wondering what Thomas knew, what he may have done.

Looking up from his coffee, Thomas hesitated. "I have some other news. That new doctor, Benjamin Elliott, was taken into custody by the Baltimore police yesterday morning soon after we docked." Snow's hand came out of his pocket empty.

"Who told the Baltimore police he was on board? He boarded late, and only two people knew." Snow made the mental correction to three, adding "There was the tobacco buyer."

Thomas nodded, sipping coffee. "A tobacco buyer, who boarded at Broome's Wharf, disembarked in a hurry when we got to Baltimore. He found two patrolmen on Light Street and brought them back to the *Northumberland*. He had quite a lot to say about Elliott and a body found on your property. The *Sun's* late edition didn't include a story of Elliott's arrest when we pulled away from the pier last night."

"I think you know something about that body yourself, Thomas."

Thomas raised his eyebrows over the rim of his cup. Snow watched Thomas place the cup back on its saucer as the silver cigar box emerged from Snow's pocket, watched Thomas sit back as Snow opened the box revealing the punched steamboat ticket.

Recovering from astonishment, Thomas snapped, "Where did you find that?"

"Where you lost it." Snow moved the silver box to his left hand, placed his right hand on the arm of the wicker setae above the hidden derringer, and waited.

Thomas blinked a few times. "I didn't have anything to do with that woman's death. Neither did Hattie."

Snow breathed in and out slowly. He thought, "How could you defend a woman who may have killed your sister?" But, he said, "How do you know that?"

Thomas leaned forward, arms on his knees. Maintaining a relaxed posture, Snow positioned the cigar case between them, reached for the coffee pot with his left hand, and filled Thomas' cup.

Thomas glanced past Snow down the central hall passage and pursed his lips. Silverware clinked on dishes as Phyllis commenced removal of breakfast from the dining room. The sounds of saws and hammers ceased. Creak and crunch of cartwheels on gravel grew louder and stopped somewhere behind the Rest. Voices, Carrie's contralto giving instructions and the Harris brothers' baritones responding, drifted indistinctly through the house.

Continuing to lean forward, Thomas spoke rapidly in a near whisper. "Hattie was hiding at Cawsin Farm. A man and woman came down Cawsin Farm Road in a pony cart. Hattie hid in the woods by the Run. The man and woman argued. The woman screamed and ran towards the woods with her clothes on fire. The man ran after her, hit her with a split of wood, and she fell. When he looked up, he saw Hattie and began chasing her with the split raised over his head. He might have caught Hattie, but the woman rose, stumbled towards the woods, and the man turned back to chase after her. That was all Hattie saw until..." Thomas broke off as Carrie came down the center hall passage in their direction.

Smiling when she saw him, Carrie began with, "Thomas, what a pleasant surprise. How good to see you. How long can you stay? I have fresh soft crabs from Bluestone Farm for lunch. Phyllis will make us..."

Her cheerful chatter ceased when, looking back and forth between the men, she took stock of their expressions. As Carrie turned to face Thomas, Snow sat back, shaking his head in a slight 'no'.

Thomas nodded and assumed his First Mate smile.

"Well, Aunt Carrie, a law clerk from Warfield and Snow wanted a special delivery to the Judge. He gave me a perfect excuse to take a morning's leave from *Northumberland* and visit you."

"Why such serious expressions?" Carrie looked back at Snow.

Thomas took a breath and decided on, "Well, I do have some disturbing news. Two Baltimore police detectives took that new doctor, Ben Elliott, into custody when we docked yesterday morning. *The Sun* may not have run the story just yet."

Carrie turned to Snow, "Do you think Freeman and the Pinkertons will know this?"

Thomas interrupted, "Not if they came down on the *Calvert* yesterday." Snow winced.

Carrie gave Thomas a sharp look. "So, you know about the fiancé and the agents?

You know when they came down to Leonardtown? You know about the body in the Run?"

Thomas caught himself with, "Buddy told me about it when Elliott boarded on Tuesday. The missing fiancée was in the papers." Carrie gazed at him with pursed lips and obvious dissatisfaction.

Phyllis appeared. Wiping her hands on an apron, she stared at Carrie and pointing back down the center hall. Snow realized he had never heard Phyllis speak, but he knew her hearing was good. Only just now, he could hear Buddy's mules and wagon coming down Snow Farm Road. The Rest didn't need ice. Snow rose and walked around the house to greet his guests taking the envelope with him. Before he reached the back yard, he had digested its content and secluded it in his overall bib pocket.

Buddy's wagon, rigged with seats for four passengers, came out from under the trees. Josiah followed on horseback. Snow hailed Sheriff Freeman, Josiah, and Buddy. Buddy tied up his mules, his passengers climbed down, and Snow introduced himself simply as William Snow. He recognized the well-dressed Pinkerton agent with the magnificent mustache and bowler hat. He had read the agent's book.

Eight years earlier, Detective Frank P. Geyer had tracked down H. H. Holmes, the infamous serial murderer of possibly hundreds, while investigating a case of life insurance fraud. After the trial and execution of Holmes, who was actually Herbert Webster Mudgett, Geyer wrote a chilling account, The Holmes-Pitezel Case; a history of the Greatest Crime of the Century.

While wondering why this famous Pinkerton arrived at the back entrance to Snow's Rest in a mule-drawn cart, Snow decided to avoid revealing the contents of his envelope. At least, he would conceal it for the present.

After escaping Carrie's interrogation, Thomas walked around the house, with his cane tucked under his arm. Snow introduced him as Thomas Coode, the first mate of *Northumberland,* here for a brief visit.

Freeman addressed Thomas. "Good to see you again, First Mate Coode. I need to talk to you before you leave." Thomas responded that he had promised Captain Geoghegan to be at Broome's Wharf when the *Northumberland* tied up. If the captain would grant leave, he would come back to see the sheriff. Freeman shifted side to side but decided not to create an issue in front of the Pinkertons. Still, Snow could tell the exchange had caught Geyer's attention.

The other two guests were a younger Pinkerton agent named Thomas Gibbon and

Gerald Ernest Rolands, fiancé of the missing Dorothea Snareborn.

Snow turned to Rolands. "I am sorry to meet you under these circumstances. Hopefully, you will find Miss Snareborn soon, and all will be well."

Rolands, who had remained aloof until this point, became agitated. "Unfortunately, that will not happen. As you know, she was found dead on your property and buried here without my permission."

Snow answered sharply. "An unknown woman found dead on Snow's Rest was buried with a funeral service on Jesuit property near here. Without identification, we did our best to honor her for her family."

Turning to Freeman, he spoke calmly. "Was Mr. Rolands able to identify the unfortunate victim found on my property from the photographs taken before her burial?"

Freeman grimaced. "Mr. Rolands seems to think the woman is his missing fiancée, Miss Snareborn. He wanted to visit the grave and the site where you found her."

Carrie approached discreetly behind Snow. To his relief, she did not invite the arrivals to lunch. Glancing at her, he noticed she was pale and wrapped in her shawl. Snow wondered what Thomas had told her, but decided to take that up with him later.

Rolands snapped. "The woman in the photographs is definitely Dorothea. According to this sheriff, she was wearing my engagement ring, and it was left here. I want it back." Sheriff Freeman stepped back, stood erect, and glared coldly at Rolands' back. Rolands blundered ahead. "After I view the gravesite, I will take steps necessary to remove Dorothea's remains to an appropriate resting place in Baltimore."

Thomas and Buddy retreated to a distance, talking in hushed tones. Snow caught one outburst from Buddy, something about not telling Sparks anything before Thomas hushed him.

Listening to Rolands rant, Snow thought, "Have her removed, claim her as your fiancée, and inherit her estate." But, he said, "I can settle your mind concerning the ring. It was left with us for safe keeping."

Rolands snapped, "Keeping is the right word for that..."

Ready to take his leave, Thomas interrupted Rolands. "I want to thank you for breakfast Judge Snow. Anytime you would like me to carry more documents for you, I will be honored to do so." Nodding to the others, Thomas barely suppressed a smile watching Rolands blanch in silence. Geyer didn't even raise an eyebrow. So, he knew.

Watching Rolands catch his breath, Snow took the silk pouch out of his pocket, retrieved the 'Dearest' ring, and offered it to him. After looking at the ring and back at Snow, he took it, examined it in his palm, and closed his hand. "Yes, this is the ring. I will bury this with Dorothea in our family cemetery."

Carrie took her cue. "Oh, I'm so sorry. That is not the ring we found on the victim's hand. There's another ring in that pouch." She took the pouch from Snow, opened it, and removed the 'Love' ring with the missing opal. Holding it out to Rolands, she added. "The ring you hold is mine. Please, may I have it back?"

Realizing the trap he had fallen into, Rolands reddened, glared at Carrie, and took a step in her direction. Freeman and Snow each took a step forward to block him. Gibbon shifted his weight stepping to Rolands' defense and finding Geyer's hand in his way, shifted back.

Rolands gave back the 'Dearest' ring and scrutinized the other. "I don't recognize that one either. Someone, whoever murdered Dorothea, has stolen her diamond engagement ring. She was lured down here by that doctor, Elliott. He probably killed her for the engagrment ring." Turning to Geyer, he demanded, "I insist you find out where they discovered her body so you can look for my ring."

Snow thought, "Inadequate recovery, too late." But, he said, "Buddy and Josiah can show you the place in the Run where we found the unidentified woman. The younger men will go on ahead, and the older men will follow."

Rolands glanced apprehensively at the Jenks. "Agents Geyer and Gibbon will accompany me. As far as these farmers are concerned, we disagree on the date Dorothea arrived. I will need protection."

Geyer didn't move or change expression when he said, "Mr. Rolands, I don't work for you. I work for the Pennsylvania Rail Road. Agent Gibbon will accompany you, and I will be along later." Josiah and Buddy started toward the path. Rolands hesitated but fell in step behind them when Gibbon joined him.

When the younger men disappeared into the woods, Snow strolled after them. Freeman and Geyer joined him, and Snow handed Freeman the letter Thomas brought that morning.

Without appearing to address either Snow or Freeman, Geyer spoke quietly. "Miss Snareborn's brother-in-law, James L. Critchen, works for the General Manager's Association hiring railroad strikebreakers. He moves around a lot, specializes in antiunion activities, and was involved in Blue Island Illinois in '94. There have been threats. The PRR asked me to investigate Dorothea's disappearance as a possible kidnapping." He held up a letter. "This letter from the School of Nursing was sent to Mr. Critchen after Miss Snareborn was reported missing by the *Sun Paper.* According to this, Miss Snareborn arranged to take an assignment in St. Mary's County on August fifth. Buddy Jenks says a nurse arrived a week earlier. Now, how can that be true?"

Snow answered while not looking in Geyer's direction. "It can be true if the nurse who arrived on July 29th was not Dorothea Snareborn." Freeman nodded in agreement.

Geyer asked, "Why would Rolands misidentify the woman in the photograph and insist that Miss Snareborn arrive a week later?" Freeman handed the letter back to Snow. Geyer glanced at it looking annoyed.

"Agent Geyer, did you have an opportunity to speak with the friend Miss Snareborn said she would visit?" Geyer grunted ascent, his annoyance increasing.

"And was that friend Elisabeth Cornman?"

Geyer stopped. "Just how the hell did you know that? We kept the friend's name out of the papers."

Snow handed Geyer back his letter along with the letter Thomas had brought from Warfield and Snow. Geyer had read it twice by the time they reached the bend in the path to Cawsin Farm where he stopped.

"How did you get this information?"

"In my experience on the bench, money and infatuation are the two most common motivations for murder. It occurred to me that the *Sun* mentioned both the birthday and the wedding date in the original headline for a reason. My law clerk, Joseph Hebb, went to the Baltimore Registrar of Wills, Harrison Rider. Harrison expedited a search for Miss Snareborn's will. As you see, it was recently changed."

"So, Miss Snareborn named Rolands as her heir before the wedding and changed it just before she disappeared?"

Snow nodded. "We don't recommend naming a fiancé as heir before a wedding. Brides and grooms do get left at the altar. Her attorneys, McGill and Philpot, would discourage it as well. But, it is done by people in love all the time."

Geyer pointed at a sum of money. "And she was to come into a substantial amount in a trust on her birthday? That would be August second, three days before the private nursing service believed she would arrive here?"

Snow nodded. "What I assume, but this document does not say, is that her sister, Mrs. Critchen, would inherit Dorothea's half of the trust if Dorothea died before her birthday on August second. After her birthday, Rolands would be the heir. Now, why Rolands misidentified the woman in the photo and tried to claim the wrong ring is still not known. He may believe he can use the letter from the Private Duty Nursing Service to discredit Buddy's assertion that Dorothea Snareborn disembarked at Broome's Wharf on July 29th. If we accept Rolands' identification and Buddy's date, Dorothea Snareborn died before her birthday. My guess is Rolands has no idea she went back to McGill and Philpot to change her will the week she disappeared. Miss Cornman signed as a witness. McGill and Philpot informed the sister of the changes after Dot was reported missing. I gather she hasn't shared that information with you or with Rolands."

Taking a deep breath and putting his forefinger and thumb to his mouth, Geyer let out an earsplitting whistle. Someone up the path whistled back, and Gibbon appeared trotting toward them followed by Rolands and the Jenks.

Geyer started back toward the mules and wagon, but Snow grabbed his arm, held his hand out for the letter. "Miss Snareborn may be alive. It is possible the woman who died here on Cawsin Farm came with a message for Elliott and was mistaken for Dot Snareborn. Elliott has been taken into custody in Baltimore based on information provided by a man who may be the murderer. We mustn't do anything that will endanger Dot Snareborn."

Geyer hesitated. He held out Snow's letter but did not let it go. "Dot Snareborn? Why did you call her Dot?"

"That is the name Ben Elliott uses, the name he came to call her by when they trained together."

Geyer rolled his eyes and nod to himself as the legs of multiple triangular relationships fell into place. "When I questioned the family, Clarissa Critchen and Gerald Rolands never looked at each other. They never gave a satisfactory explanation for failing to report Snareborn missing." He held up the School of Nursing letter. "Neither of them mentioned Elliott or private duty nursing until after this letter arrived addressed to her husband. Rolands was stunned, even glared at Clarissa Critchen. It was the woman who blushed. She obviously had knowledge of Snareborn's plans and hadn't told anyone or at least anyone in the family." Snow and Freeman glanced at each other taking in Geyer's implication that someone else was involved, someone Clarissa Critchen hired to murder her sister.

When Gibbon, Rolands, and the Jenks caught up with them, Geyer said they needed to board the *Northumberland* when she docked. He wasn't staying the night and sailing back to Leonardtown with Freeman. As they reached the mules and wagon, Snow added the steamer had whistle her approach to Porto Bello across the river. The Jenks gave him a questioning look, but went along with the ruse. Rolands objected to the sudden departure but followed rather than get left behind.

As the mules started down Snow's Rest Road in a reluctant trot, Carrie's contralto reached him from the porch. "Judge Snow, I do believe you have told a lie." He turned to see her smiling at him. "I can't say I'm unhappy to see them go."

Snow handed Carrie the letter. He scrutinized her expression and waited for her response. "So, she's alive. She couldn't have been in the office of McGill and Philpot signing a will and getting off a steamer at Broome's Wharf on the same day. Who is the Mary in the photograph, and why was she murdered?"

"I don't know. At this point, I am only conjecturing. I wouldn't be surprised if she were a victim of mistaken identity. Buddy said he remembered her dress. He said his wife would like that dress. You pointed out that it was very well made, but not Mary's because it didn't fit."

Carrie nodded. "Well, William Snow, you are going to find out who Mary was. Come with me. You get cleaned up, and I'll pack a carpet bag for you." On their way through the kitchen, Carrie told Phyllis to take a message to Travis. They needed the pony and cart ready at the house, ready in less than ten minutes.

Phyllis whispered, "Yes, Mam." and ran to find her husband.

Snow commented, "I thought she couldn't speak."

"She speaks to her husband in a whisper and sometimes to others if she knows them well. Poor dear had a terrible childhood."

Upstairs, Carrie marched into the master bedroom and pulled a carpet bag from under the bed. She packed linens from the dresser and clothes from the oak wardrobe. Snow considered reminding her he was returning to a home with clean clothes but decided he enjoyed having her in the room. He stripped to his waist, ran a wet sponge over his chest, and a hand over the shadow of his emerging whiskers. All the while, Carrie pretend not to look at him. Surrendering to impulse, he took two quick strides across the room, spun her toward him and lifted her in one movement. They held each other in the embrace of a passionate kiss and he flopped her over on the bed. She pummeled his back in mock resistance.

Breaking away from his kiss, she giggled like a girl. "William Snow, do you think you can kiss a girl once and take advantage?"

He grinned back. "I can always hope." They stared into each other's eyes, knowing time was against them in many ways. He said, "Come. Come to Baltimore, even if just for a visit. When you finish packing all these things you think I should take, come with them to see they are delivered properly. Make that your excuse, if you need one." Her smile faded, her expression cooled, and the woman returned.

They heard the nervous pony snorting in the back yard as Travis backed it between shafts of the cart. Snow rolled away and the bed springs creaked. They heard Phyllis treading heavily up the stairs, clearing her throat.

Carrie called out to her. "We'll be down directly, Phyllis. Thank Travis and ask him to hold her until we get there."

Phyllis returned to her soft tread hurrying down the stairs. Snow grinned down at Carrie, stood, and lifted her. She rearranged her skirt and glanced past him at something in the room. Snow dressed quickly and took his derby hat from the top shelf of the wardrobe. Carrie hastily finished packing, lifted the carpet-bag, and started down the stairs.

Snow stopped in the library at the gun cabinet, retrieved his Pocket Pistol, and started down behind her. "You can have the derringer. If you are going to travel alone around the county, you may need it. It is on the front porch behind the spittoon."

Looking up at him from the center hall, she smiled. "No, it's not. I took it already."

Taking a quick glance back up the stairs, Snow suddenly knew what she had looked at in the master bedroom. He climbed back up to retrieve Dorothea's copy of <u>Notes On Nursing</u> and the silver cigar case from the night table. When he arrived in the center hall, he took the bag from Carrie and placed the book with the photograph in among the clothes. On the way through the center hall, Snow deviated into the front parlor to take a handful of cigars and what remained of his Jenks Best. By the time they reached the back porch, he realized she had not answered his question then realized he had not asked one.

In the yard, Travis held the stomping pony. Sensing urgency, it pawed up dust as Snow lifted the carpet bag and stepped up into the cart. Turning he held out his hand to lift Carrie up, but she stepped back.

Withdrawing his hand, Snow stood in the cart while Travis held the eager pony.

"Will you come...please?" There, finally, he had asked.

A range of emotion crossed her face before she answered, "I will think on it." A steamship issued one short blast from across the river, indicating she was leaving Porto Bello for Broomes Wharf. "You better get along if you are planning to meet the *Northumberland.*"

Carrie nodded to Travis who climbed up on the driver's seat and released the pony to step out in a brisk trot. Snow sat to avoid falling and waved. She hesitated before lifting her hand. As the cart slipped under an arc of wooded limbs, Snow glanced back, but Carrie had turned away.

Linda A. Stewart

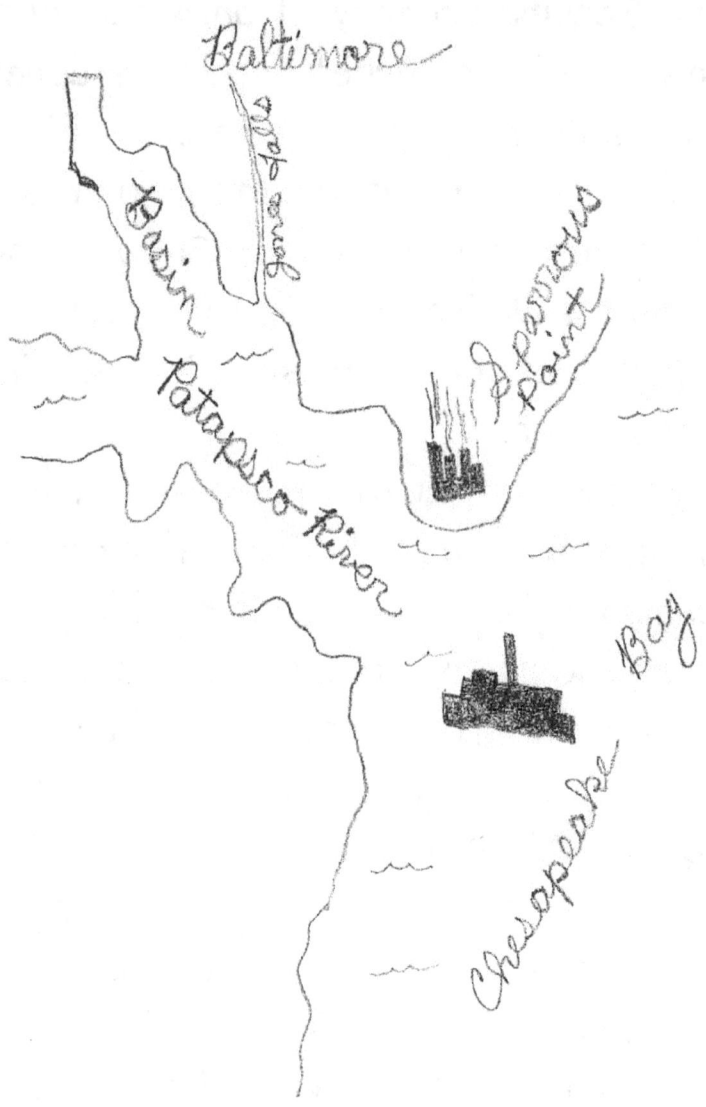

Chapter 12: A Run Up the Bay

Something told the wild geese
It was time to fly,
Summer sun was on their wings,
Winter in their cry.
    Rachel Fields (1894 – 1942)

Gleaming white in late afternoon sun, *Northumberland* nestled beside Bromes Wharf. Vacationers returning from Piney Point to Baltimore occupied most of the staterooms. A slight whiff of gray drifted from her towering smokestack as the crew prepared for her run up the Bay. Launched by the Weems line only three years earlier, she was unrivaled for luxury among the overnight packets on the Baltimore and Washington route.

As the pony trotted briskly down Brome's Wharf Road, a first billow of smoke preceding the steamer's whistled warning of departure. Snow was relieved to see Thomas Coode overseeing the loading of cargo. Thomas responded to Snow's wave and signaled deckhands to delay removing the gangway. Snow alighted, and Travis followed with the carpetbag leaving the pony to search out a convenient mouthful of grass.

At the foot of the ramp, Snow turned to Travis and handed him a three cent nickel. "Travis, if someone needed a carriage or cart, would he be able to get the loan of one at Bromes Store?"

"Well, might depend on if they know you. They has dories and catboats for rent. A few horses, mules, wagons and such. Like this one." Travis glanced at the coin taking care to disguise his displeasure over the unpopular coinage.

Snow headed down the dock to the steamer. After thanking Thomas for waiting, he boarded and paid the $2.75 cent first class passage.

"Judge, I thought you might be coming, so I saved a forward stateroom on the port side next to the Pinkertons. The other man, Rolands, insisted on a last-minute change to an aft cabin on starboard away from them. I can put you on either side."

"Thank you, Thomas. I'll take the starboard side near Rolands to keep an eye on him." Thomas spoke to a steward, and Snow was taken around to his stateroom. The *Northumberland* gave one short blast before dock hands threw off her lines. A puff of smoke preceded the gentle slide of her 300-foot hull aft into the river.

Thomas went forward to check white lights on the fore and aft masts that indicated bow or stern to an approaching ship. Two white lights visible at night, one 15 feet above the other, indicated a steamer's bow ahead and coming towards you. With the smoke stack between the masts, the forward mast was hidden from view of traffic astern. One white light visible at night indicated a ship's stern ahead. Thomas came along the starboard deck to inspect a lantern that threw red light from straight ahead to two compass points abaft of beam. After nodding to Snow who stood by the rail, Thomas passed around to port for inspection of a green lantern. Through all the work of getting underway, Thomas barely limped.

Above them the year's first spearheaded line of Canada geese winged their way south, beating the eternal change of season. Guided by their collective memory of tens of thousands of journeys, the geese signaled their passage down the Bay with a cacophony of honking as *Northumberland's* two short blasts signaled her intended passage down St. Mary's River.

The steamer backed a slow arc to port, her water line came parallel to the shore, and she proceeded south in 20 feet of water. Avoiding shallows of less than a foot at Windmill and Priest's Points, Captain Geoghegan navigated his ship down river. After Cornfield Harbor, he turned the helm over to the ship's pilot. From the window of his cabin, Snow admired the professional routine, felt the gliding motion.

While they eased down St. Mary's River, a haze rose ahead over the Potomac in the cooling late afternoon air. For the first six nautical miles, the *Northumberland* made less than half her maximum speed out of caution to avoid shoals along the river banks. An hour later, they steamed past St. George's Bar, made several slow corrections southeast, and surged forward into smooth waters on the Potomac. By the time they rounded Point Lookout, water depth fell away to over 40 feet, and she made 10 knots. A half gale coming up the Bay cleared the haze but whipped up a chop that promised an uncomfortable night for anyone lacking sea legs.

Although the wash stand provided hot and cold running water for his needed shave, Snow decided to wait for calmer seas. Foregoing a meal of tongue sandwiches offered by the steward, he ordered graham crackers in warm milk with a bottle of spring water. Then he settled into the comfortable bed and fell asleep rocked by the ship's rolling motion.

Hours later, one long blast from the whistle woke Snow an hour later as *Northumberland* signaled port to port passage with another ship. The gale had subsided. Somewhere to port, another ship answered. A series of signals passed indicating the vessels would come along side and exchange passengers or cargo. Although he had seen this done many times, it was always fascinating to watch.

While he prepared to go on deck for the spectacle, he felt the ship lose way. Her bow corrected to starboard, she drifted into an arc, and the remaining winds push her stern around. Snow moved a chair from his luxury stateroom out to the deck and lit a cigar. Through gathering dusk, one white light above the *Virginia's* stern was visible ahead. A vessel the Baltimore, Chesapeake, and Atlantic Railway Company put into service that spring, she rivaled the *Northumberland* in luxury. Now she lay just ahead, head to wind with enough way on to control the helm. The *Northumberland* approached her with just enough way on to come alongside before reducing power. Lines passed securing them bow and stern, and they fell together, gangway to gangway. The two massive hulls became one. Several passengers from the *Northumberland* who were bound for Fredericksburg, Virginia moved across the gangway followed by their luggage. Staring into gathering gloom, Snow suddenly stood and knocked his chair over. The whole event took only minutes, each steamer signaled a short blast, and they fell away. The *Virginia* had steamed her way south into night by the time Snow reached Thomas out on deck.

Thomas responded to Snow's astonished expression. "Rolands purchased a ticket from the purser and walked across the gangway without his luggage. I had no way to stop him. Why is he suddenly changing course to Virginia?"

Snow shrugged and lowered his voice. "Did Hattie describe the man at Cawsin Farm? Could he have been Rolands?"

Thomas hesitated, seemed to weigh his response. "She described the man as dark, large, and strong. At first, she hid. Then she was frightened and running from him. Rolands is slight and sandy haired. The man at Cawsin Farm is not the type to run away."

Snow thought Thomas' answer speculative, but that sliver of information did point away from Rolands and toward Sparks. "Is Geyer aware yet?" Thomas shook his head. "Then, I'll tell him Rolands is gone myself. Where is their stateroom?" Thomas directed a cabin boy escort Snow around to the Pinkerton's port side cabin as *Northumberland* made a gradual turn back up the Bay.

Snow found the agents deep into a game of high low poker with two other passengers. Gibbon offered Snow a whiskey, and they both sat back as Geyer proceeded to win half the last pot with the low hand.

Geyer showed his hand, stretched, and addressed his adversaries. "Gentlemen, you won some, and I won some. Now, I have business with the Judge. Would you please excuse us?" The two passengers inspected Snow with interest as they reluctantly left into the night.

Gibbon stood in the opened door as the card players walked down the deck toward their staterooms. When their distance was sufficient, he turned to Geyer who nodded. Gibbon closed the door and took his seat.

Snow began with, "You didn't invite Mr. Rolands to join your game? Surely he had some money to lose."

Gibbon shook his head. "He has a reputation at cards. We couldn't find anyone who accused him of cheating. Just has a good head for it." Geyer glared at Gibbon. Gibbon squirmed in his chair.

Snow nodded and turned to Geyer. "How closely did you track the whereabouts of Gerald Rolands and James Critchen during the week of July 29th? How closely are you watching Rolands tonight?"

Geyer hesitated before answering. "Well, they both work for PRR, so it was easy to determine if they were at work that day..." Realization spread across his face, he sat back slack-jawed and stared at Snow. "Rolands changed ships? He ran?"

Anger rose in his voice. "Where is that ship headed?"

"South to Fredericksburg."

Silence stretch on as Geyer regained control. "PRR will decide if the Pinkerton Agency is sent to find Rolands. Our task was to determine if Miss Snareborn was a kidnap victim. She was not. I can stretch that assignment to finding where she is presently and to discovering the identity of the woman found on your property."

Snow pressed him. "So, you haven't looked into where Rolands and Critchen were on July 29th?"

Geyer nodded in Gibbon's direction. "Tom, you can tell Judge Snow."

Gibbon sat up and recited his findings. "Agent Geyer sent me to interview railroad employees who work with and for James Critchen. Critchen and Rolands were at work every work day during the last two weeks in July. Critchen reported Miss Snareborn missing on August fourth, so I did not ask about dates after that day. On the weekends, only Critchen and Rolands who would know each other's whereabouts. Although, Rolands worked in the office and yards most Saturdays. And now, apparently, we don't have Rolands."

Geyer observed, "Well, he's guilty of something, or he knows something."

"Or he is afraid of someone." Snow responded.

Geyer gave Snow a shrewd glance. "I think you know who he is afraid of."

Snow nodded. "At this point, possibly James Critchen if there is an affair between Rolands and Mrs. Critchen. Or possibly, whomever murdered the woman found in Snow's Run. There are a few pieces of information I can provide that lead to another possible suspect in that death. However, that person has no motive, and the evidence is circumstantial." Then he told Geyer about Albert M. Sparks; his connection with Moore's Tobacco, his arrival on July 29th, and his actions resulting in Ben Elliott's arrest. Holding back the Moore's Turkish wrapper found at Cawsin Farm, Snow summarized his conclusions. "We don't know of any connection between Sparks and Rolands or Critchen. In addition, we do not know for certain what connection the woman who arrived on July 29th has with Miss Snareborn."

Snow weighed telling Geyer about that copy of <u>Notes On Nursing</u> and the photograph but decided to delay. Instead, he made a request. "Would it be possible for you and Mr. Gibbon to find and question Sparks when we land in Baltimore tomorrow? I will go to the School of Nursing and discover if they have heard from Miss Snareborn since your departure to St. Mary's."

Geyer pursed his lips in thought. "After I wire my findings to the Pinkerton office in Philadelphia, we will look for Sparks at

Moore's Tobacco. If he's there, we'll question him concerning Dr. Elliott, Miss Snareborn, and his actions on July 29th. We'll watch his reaction. But that's about as far as we can get..." A soft footfall and creak of deck boards sounded outside the cabin door.

Gibbon took one silent stride to the door, jerked it open, surveyed the deck in both directions, and glanced back at Geyer. "Just ship's crew on deck."

Still staring suspiciously at the closed door, Geyer finished with, "...involved. It is not clear to me why you focused on this buyer as a suspect."

Snow took a gamble, pulled the cigar band from his pocket, and placed it on the table. He watched Geyer for a reaction. It was Gibbon who showed surprise and flattened the band to better view the locomotive pictured there.

Snow turned to him. "Do you know anyone who smokes these?"

Gibbon glanced at Geyer for guidance. Geyer prompted him with "Where have you seen this?"

Gibbon responded, "James Critchen smokes them. Offered me one on my first visit before you arrived from Philadelphia." He went to his carpet bag, opened it, took out his cigar case, and produced a Moore's Turkish. "His wife, Clarissa, gave him a box for their second anniversary. So, the connection may be Clarissa Critchen." Geyer turned to Snow with an expectant look.

Snow decided to keep information to a minimum. "A discarded band like this one was found in the kitchen house of Cawsin Farm. Evidence of a disturbance and a recent fire in the stove leads to possibilities. These cigars aren't sold at Brome's Wharf store, but Sparks gives them away to growers he favors. Buddy saw him at the wharf on July 29th. Sparks may have given cigars away and may remember who he gave them to that day. Now that we know a connection between him and the Critchens, it raises possibilities they are involved. Buddy Jenks says Sparks gambles, loses, and owes money."

Geyer patted his mustache. "It could just be a coincidence that Mrs. Critchen bought Moore's Turkish cigars."

Snow countered, "There are over 500 cigar factories in Baltimore. You're a gambling man, Frank. What are the odds of that coincidence?"

Geyer raised an eyebrow and nodded in agreement. "We'll find and question Sparks. Another coincidence. Moore and Sparks are the last names of two men hung by vigilantes after the Jeffersonville, Madison, and Indianapolis Railroad robbery in 1868. That one heist netted the Reno Brother's Gang $96,000. The money was never recovered. On the strength of that coincidence, I won't have any difficulty getting permission from the Pennsylvania office to pursue and question Albert Sparks."

Snow remembered the Reno Brothers Gang and had followed their crimes in newspapers during the 1860s. However, he could not recall that level of detail. Although a youth when that robbery took place, Geyer was a Pinkerton, their best.

"How old were you in 1868?"

"Oh, probably fifteen, sixteen." Geyer smiled knowing he impressed the Judge. "Well, Gibbon and I will need a few hours of sleep if we are going to track down Mr. Sparks tomorrow."

Gibbon held up the lantern and stepped out the door, letting light shine out ahead of them. After scrutinizing the deck, he offered to escort Snow to his stateroom. Snow declined and went back down the deck hopeful of a few hours' sleep tonight, hopeful of finding Dorothea Snareborn and Albert Sparks tomorrow. As he rounded the rear observation deck toward his cabin, he found Thomas at the rail smoking a Little Van Bibber and joined him.

After a few moments, Snow asked, "What made you think I would make the run up the bay tonight?"

"You found my cigar case. So, you've been looking for someone."

"Thomas, do you know where she is?"

Thomas stared off into the night until Snow thought he wouldn't answer. Finally, Thomas said, "I did. But, she's gone again. After taking her to Baltimore, I put her up in a respectable ladies residence near mine. A week later, I came back from a run, and she had disappeared."

Questions sprang up in Snow's mind. Where was the money Paul and Hattie took from the tunnel below Snow's Rest? Did Hattie still possess his Colt revolver? What happened to the medical bag and the letter? He asked, "Did she have a medical bag? Did she carry a letter of recommendation?"

Thomas turned to look at Snow and blinked a few times. "She had the bag. I don't know of any letter."

Snow nodded and left it at that. Either Thomas failed to look through Hattie's things or he held his cards close. Snow found Thomas' motivations difficult to understand. A feeling of increasing unease settled over him as he took his stub of the Moore's Turkish back to his stateroom.

At sunrise, *Northumberland* gave two short blasts signaling her intent to overtake and pass the port side of another vessel. The bawling of cattle drifted across the water from the smaller steamer. Through dissipating fog, hog's heads of tobacco gradually appeared on its deck. Tracks of the Washington, Potomac and Chesapeake Railroad Company only serviced northern St. Mary's County. The rails terminated at Mechanicsville, half way down the Southern Maryland peninsula, making transportation by water indispensable for farmers shipping to markets in Washington and Baltimore.

Snow rose and gazed out his window into visibility of about a half mile in fog. He felt a correction of the helm to port three ship lengths past the smaller vessel. After the rounding into Patapsco River just south of Bodkin Neck, Snow signaled the cabin steward and ordered coffee with toast delivered to his stateroom. He washed, shaved, and dressed before it arrived. With the carpet bag and the last of his coffee, he proceeded to the forward observation deck. He reminded himself to thank Carrie for packing clean clothes. Then it occurred to him. When would he see her again? He stared into his coffee, watching its vapors rise into cool morning air.

Steaming up the Patapsco River towards Baltimore Harbor, they corrected to port again as Sparrows Point came into view in dissipating fog. The standard of a new destiny unfurled above them. Where once peach orchards ripened their succulent fruit in summer sun, the Pennsylvania Steel Company wantonly belched billowing smoke, an unfurling pennant to progress. Fierce as a savage starving dog, the mill sprawled over the soft body of land, breaking it, devouring it, suppressing it. Undefeated by the Panic of '93, the steel men rose, bare-fisted fighters flinging punches of red hot ingots into the world. They held up their prize in brawling, sweating arms, the prize of Baltimore, the nation's third-largest port with $130 million in foreign trade. Snow only gazed with melancholy and alienation at this rising ensign to change.

Linda A. Stewart

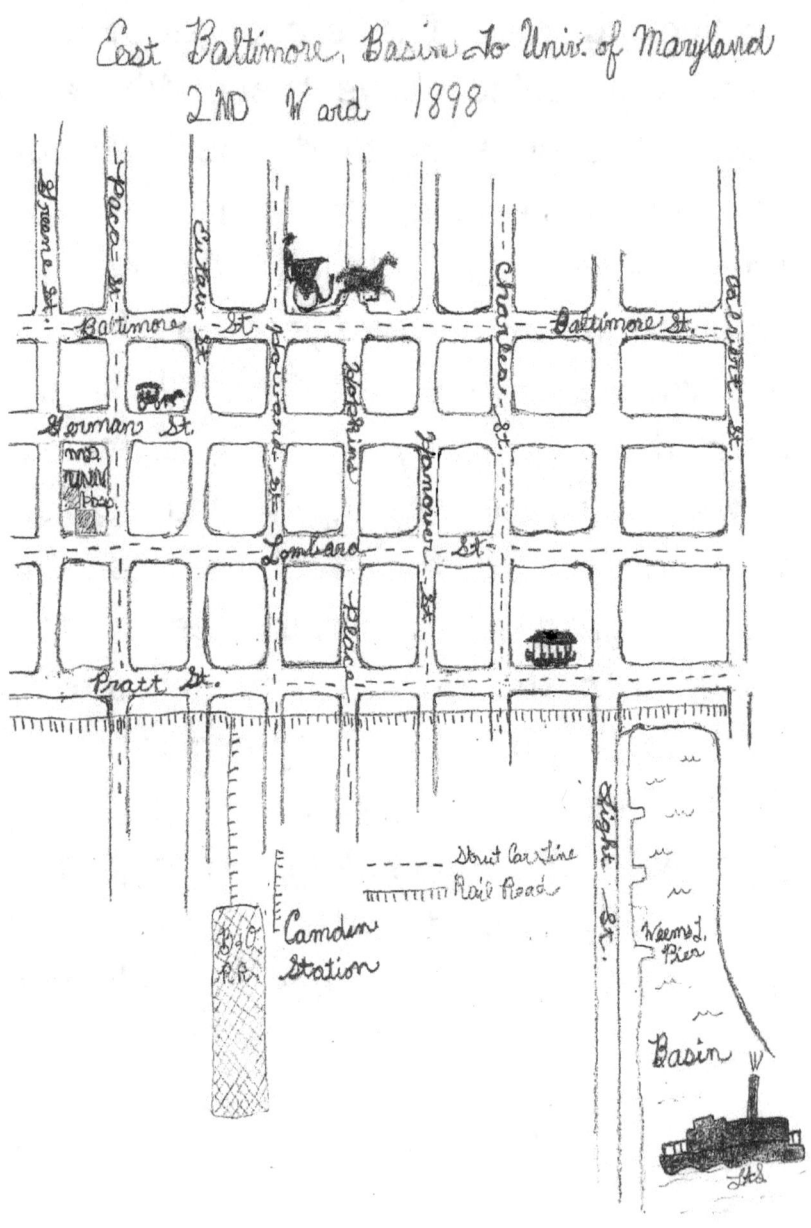

East Baltimore, Basin to Univ. of Maryland
2ND Ward 1898

Baltimore St.   Baltimore St.
German St.
Lombard St.   Hanover St.
Pratt St.

- - - Street Car Line
▯▯▯▯▯ Rail Road

Camden
Station

B&O
R.R.

Weems L.
Pier

Basin

Chapter 13: The Search

All truths are easy to understand once they are discovered; the point is to discover them.
  Galileo Galilei (1564-1642)

Snow's thoughts turned to arranging a meeting with Thomas later that day, but a search of the deck proved disappointing. The Pinkerton's closed cabin door might mean they had already disembarked. As Snow walked down the port side gangway, he handed a nickel and a letter to a cabin boy. From the dock, he watched the cabin door open to the boy's knock. Geyer opened the letter instructing the Pinkerton to leave any messages at the offices of Warfield and Snow. Then Snow was gone.

Along the pier men and beasts moved in purposeful activity so that the inaction of that one observer made him conspicuous.

Dressed in tweeds and a new Homburg hat, the observer stood out from sweating dock workers, carpenters laden with tools, and lorry drivers delivering shipments. Knowing Spark's wait futile, Snow wondered if he would follow Rolands into *Virginia*. Then again, he wondered if Sparks would even risk exposing himself by asking after Rolands' whereabouts. Snow walked down the pier in the opposite direction, his back to Sparks. Then he crossed the pier and walked behind Sparks unobserved. At the new terminal and headquarters of the Baltimore Steam Packet Company, Snow glanced back. The distant figure still surveyed passengers disembarking from *Northumberland*.   Thomas   Coode's uniformed figure was nowhere to be found in the mayhem.

Instead of taking a Hansom cab, Snow decided to take a streetcar. A new twelve bench open summer car built by G. J. Brill company came along in less than 5 minutes, and he took it north on Light Street getting off at Baltimore Street. There he walked one block east, turned north on Charles, stepped into a doorway, and waited five minutes checking for Sparks or Gibbon. Once he was satisfied, he hired another Hansom cab and drew the shades down. Then, he directed the driver through a zigzag route to University Hospital and the School Of Nursing on the corner of Greene St. and Lombard Avenue.

Alighting from the cab with his carpet bag, Snow paid for this leg of his journey. Then he directed the cab driver to wait an hour and added a generous tip to insure compliance. As an afterthought, he asked the driver to remember passengers in any cabs that might pass by successively or wait at curbside within line of sight.

Snow enter the Lombard Avenue entrance of University Hospital and walked through gardens of the central courtyard. After doubling back, he disappeared into the School of Nursing. He hoped for an appointment with the Superintendent of Nurses. Her secretary told him Mrs. Taylor was on rounds in the Lying In Department. The nature of services provided there made it impossible to predict her return. While deciding between waiting and leaving his card, a thought occurred to him. The secretary might provide information if he worded the request carefully. First, he wrote a note requesting an appointment with Mrs. Taylor on his calling card and handed it to the secretary. Observing a change in her demeanor, he asked his question.

"Also, a Miss Elisabeth Cornman visited our offices recently and failed to leave an address. We have an item that was left behind. It may belong to her, or she may know the owner. Would it be possible for you to provide an address so my law clerk can contact her?"

"Yes, Judge Snow, I think we can provide that information." The secretary consulted an index card file, copied information on a fresh card, and handed Snow two address for Elisabeth Cornman. Elated, Snow thanked her and requested an appointment with Mrs. Taylor on Monday. He received one for 11:00 AM, after rounds and before lunch.

Then, just as he was leaving, he asked her one more question. "I have a photograph of nurses taken in the men's ward here at University Hospital. It was left with us. Could you identify this woman?" Taking the photograph from his bag, he pointed.

The secretary stepped back and paused. Snow waited, then asked, "Is this Dorothea Snareborn?" The secretary made a slight nod. "And this woman? Is her first name is Mary."

The secretary peered at the face. "Yes, that is Mary Flannery. She left the hospital some time ago. She just didn't show up for work."

"At about the time that Miss Snareborn disappeared?"

The secretary blinked, stared away as if thinking about that coincidence for the first time, and nodded again. "Now that you mention it, yes, the same week." Hurriedly, she included, "If you wait here, I will find Mrs. Taylor. She may want to see you today."

"Thank you, but I have another appointment. If Mrs. Taylor has anything she would like to tell me, she should call my office and leave a message. I will be there later today."

Pleased with his success, Snow retreated to the courtyard and took care to exit through the Greene Street entrance. Approaching his cab from behind, he saw Pinkerton Agent Gibbon talking to the driver. At that moment a street Arabber cart loaded with fruit pulled to curbside blocking Gibbon from view. Snow turned his back to Gibbon and reached into his coat pocket. With a shiny silver dime of Liberty wearing a laurel wreath, Snow prepared to delay the Arabber's departure by haggling over a purchase. A hand reached down and snatched the dime. Snow looked up into a familiar face.

Snow's boyhood friend, John Benjamin Lundy leaned over, smiling at his own chicanery. He suggested Snow step into the cart, sit among crates of peaches, and exchange his derby hat for the stained farmer's straw hidden among watermelons. After removing his jacket, Snow turned to face the opposite side of the Greene Street from his waiting cab. The elderly, gray at the bit pony clopped its way north on Greene through the busy Lombard Avenue intersection. John gleefully sang "peeeches, cannntilope, waaatermelon" and the harness bells jingled. Gibbon never looked. Snow smiled recalling Carrie's comment that we don't see what we're not looking for. With that sobering thought, he wondered who else he had not seen following him on Light Street.

John urged his pony through traffic north on Greene then east on Baltimore. Snow waited until they were around the corner before changing back into his derby hat, and speaking to John. "How are you and Sarah?"

At first, John just shook his head. Halfway down the block, he assured Snow, "We getting by." Snow slipped two Liberty Head five dollar gold pieces from is pocket.

Knowing John to be a man of few words, Snow got to the point, "How did you know where to find me? Did Travis follow me up from St. Mary's and tell you I was coming?"

John glanced back in surprise. "Travis Harris? No, First Mate Thomas Coode come by this morning. Told me to keep an eye on you, keep you off Lombard and Charles."

Revelations fell like ripe fruit in an orchard when gale winds sweep up the Bay. Snow thought of all the cigar factories along Charles Street and wondered where Moore's Tobacco was located. Perhaps, Thomas had also seen Sparks waiting on Light Street Pier. Lastly, he wondered how long it would take Geyer to send his telegram before searching for Sparks. He said, "Give my regards to Sarah. I am so sorry for your loss of Paul. We enjoyed his music nightly at the Rest." Snow reached over the cart seat and left the gold pieces. John nodded without looking back.

Snow grew increasingly impatient with the slow pace of the ancient pony. At the corner of German Street and Eutaw, he alighted from John's cart and hired another Hansom. After a wave to John, he directed the cab north at a pace that would get him to an address on Howard

Street before Pinkerton Agent Gibbon. Mrs. Taylor's secretary had provided Snow with this address, a respectable residence for nurses working at Maryland General Hospital. Snow thought of Poe's <u>The Purloined Letter</u> and decided a boarding house full of nurses was the perfect place to hide Dorothea Snareborn.

Reaching Linden Avenue, Snow directed the cab to stop north at the corner of Read Street. He removed <u>Notes On Nursing</u> from the carpetbag along with the Pocket Pistol. After concealing the later in his inside jacket pocket, he left the carpet bag in the cab. Then he paid the driver double and directed him to wait east at Read and Howard. With the Hansom out of sight, Snow walked south to Maryland General and then through the grounds to Howard Street. As he walked south on Howard, another Hansom trotted past and stopped. Several steps later, Snow looked over his shoulder. One man in a dark suit and Homburg hat, the cab's passenger, walked slowly north away from him.

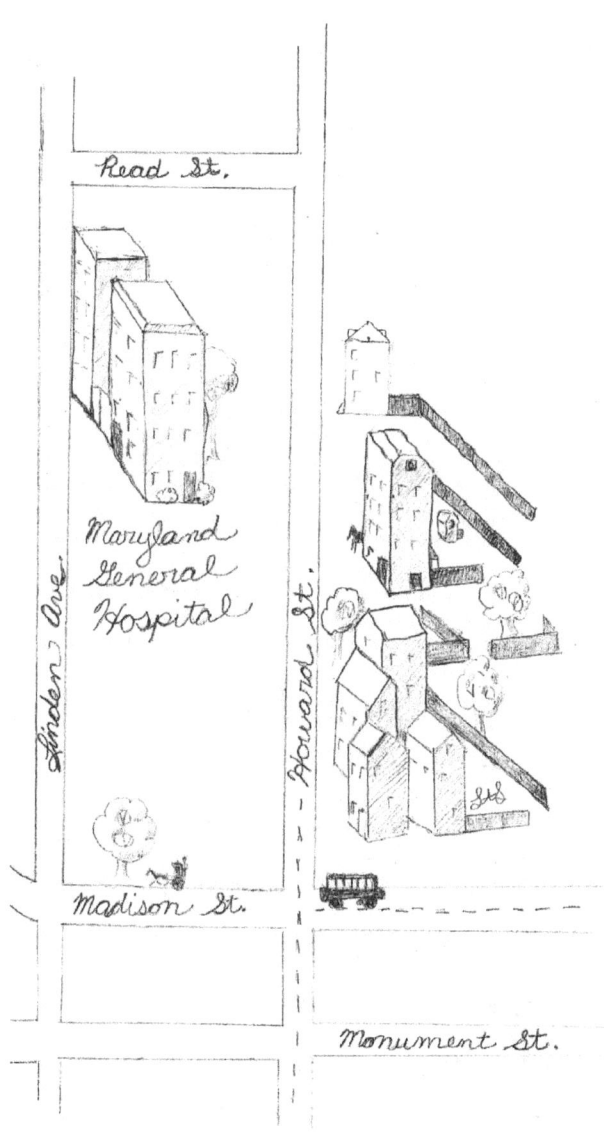

In the other direction, several passengers alighted from a streetcar at Madison and Howard. One man wore a business suit. One woman carried a basket of clean laundry. Another man man carried a tool box and walked with a cane. Snow doubled back to the Howard Street Nurses Residence and walked up the steps to the wraparound porch. On reaching the last wooden step below the porch, he heard a horse snort somewhere along the side of the house. Retreating down two steps, he spotted the forehead of a well-groomed and braided carriage horse standing along the side of the house. He mounted the stairs to the door.

Unbuttoning the last button of his jacket, Snow held his derby in his left hand to conceal the bulge in his pocket. He tucked the book under his left arm allowing his right hand freedom for a handshake or a pistol, whichever was required. A glance up and down the street told him the

Homburg had vanished. The streetcar passengers dispersed down allies leading to servant entrances at the rear of houses. While the door latch clicked open, Snow took a calling card from his pocket and held it lightly in his right hand.

As expected, an aging butler in jacket and gloves answered the door. Another man stood well behind in the hall just to the left. Snow presented a relaxed, amiable posture, showed the butler his card, and asked for Miss Elisabeth Cornman. Behind the butler, Baltimore City Police Sergeant Evans stepped forward and directed Snow be admitted. Deeper in the house, voices were raised, voices in contention. Snow stepped into the foyer.

The Sergeant greeted him with, "Judge Snow, please wait here in the hall. I will tell Police Commissioner Upsher you are here." The sergeant stepped into the front parlor, and the butler stood expectantly beside Snow. After Snow declined to relinquish his derby, the butler observed the bulk under the jacket and retreated to the servant hall. Not waiting to be announced, Snow followed the sergeant into the parlor.

"Good morning Miss Cornman, Commissioner Upsher, I am here to represent Miss Cornman and Miss Snareborn." He handed his calling card to Miss Cornman who sat alone on a settee and shook the surprised commissioner's hand. Turning to the maid, who stood by the sideboard in a black dress, white apron, and lace cap, he gestured to the empty place beside Elisabeth Cornman. "Miss Snareborn, will you join us?"

Evans and Upsher looked at each other with astonishment. Without being told, Evans retreated through the door, pushed it partially shut and stood where he could observe both the front room and the parlor. Placing the book on his knees as he sat down, Snow covered it and the bulge in his pocket with his derby.

Commissioner Upsher addressed Miss Cornman angrily with, "Well, that answers my question as to the whereabouts of Miss Snareborn."

Catching a warning glance from Snow, Upsher moderated his tone. "Miss Snareborn, I am glad to find you well. There are questions that need answering."

Snow raised a hand cutting him off. "Miss Cornman and Miss Snareborn, first I want to assure you that with Commissioner Upsher, Sergeant Evans, and myself present, you are safe from harm." Watching tears well up in Dot's eyes, he waited while she regained her composure before making his request. "Doctor Elliott is in custody, and you may be able to arrange his release. Please tell us why you went into hiding, why you are pretending to be Mary Flannigan."

Dorothea sat beside Elisabeth, took a deep breath, and wiped her eyes on a handkerchief embroidered MAF. "This is all so awful. Mary was trying to escape a brutal father and brother. They beat her, made her work two jobs, and took her wages. One night, she came to the ward late. She was limping. Later, she fell asleep in the privy." Turning to smile at Elisabeth, she continued, "We woke her, and she confided in us. She pleaded with us not to tell the charge nurse she had fallen asleep. She was working all day here at the Nurses Residence and all night at University Hospital." Elisabeth put a comforting arm around Dorothea's shoulder. "That same day I discovered my half-sister, Clarissa, in the arms of my fiancé. I went to the dressmaker for a fitting and intended to shop for new gloves afterwards. Instead, I returned early. Gerald's hat and gloves lay on the foyer table. I thought he would be in the front parlor waiting for me. The parlor was empty. As I went up to change into my nurse's uniform for evening rounds, I heard the unmistakable sounds of gasping, moans, and rustling clothes from inside the closed library. I tried to open the door. It was locked, and the noises stopped. At that moment, I just knew. I went down to the kitchen and directed a maid to fetch my gloves, saying I left them in the library. She refused. Everyone knew."

Upsher said, "She is your half-sister?"

Snow raised his hand and waited for Dorothea to finish.

She took a deep breath. "Elisabeth invited me to stay with her until after my birthday. When I returned from evening rounds, I told Clarissa that I would take time off from the hospital to visit Elisabeth for a few days. Then, I packed my clothes and left."

Snow silently contemplated her story for several minutes and then inquired,

"And you had previously changed your will to benefit Mr. Rolands in anticipation of your wedding?" She nodded. "So, you went to stay with Miss Cornman and made an appointment to change your beneficiary?"

"Yes. But I didn't tell Clarissa or Gerald I would do that."

Upsher interrupted, "And you took your nurse's black medical bag?"

Dot nodded. At that point, Elisabeth interrupted. "The next day, I asked the Private Duty Nursing service if they had any referrals Mary Flannigan might fill. They said they only referred alumnus of the School of Nursing, but they did have one difficulty to fill request from a doctor in a southern county. When I discovered it was Ben Elliott, well, he was sweet on Dot. So I got the idea to have Dot agree to the referral and send Mary instead. We wrote Ben a letter explaining the plan and gave it to Mary. Dot would join them later, after her birthday. Mary would be impossible to find if she was taking Dot's place."

Snow leaned forward, quietly addressing Dot. "That doesn't explain why you took a position here as parlor maid."

Dot closed her eyes. "After I left my sister's house, I had one more evening of rounds at University Hospital. At the end of rounds, we all came out to hail a cab. There was one cab I liked to take. The driver was friendly, and he usually waited for me. That night it was different."

Elisabeth described that night's events. "There was another cab instead, one we had never seen before. The driver didn't look or act like a cab driver. He hailed Dot and cut in front of another cab. Mary was going with us, and she stepped toward the cab first, but I pulled her back. Something was wrong. So, we went back into the hospital. The cab went down the block and waited where he could see both the Lombard and Greene entrances. We went out through the School of Physics and took a street car to my parent's house. Later that night, the same cab passed by my parent's home several times and waited up the street. I know it was the same because the horse had white front stockings all the way up to its front knees. I was to move to the Howard Street Nurses Residence the next day to begin an assignment at Maryland General. They needed a new parlor maid as Mary left without warning. We had dressed Mary up as Dot, so we dressed Dot up as a parlor maid." She hugged Dot. "Later we discovered that Mary had left for St. Mary's County a week earlier than she was supposed to. We were very surprised at the fuss in the papers over Dot's disappearance. Until the news of Ben Elliott's arrest appeared in the <u>Sun Paper</u> this morning, we had no idea that poor Mary was dead. This is just awful." The young women cried and hugged each other.

Commissioner Upsher looked through the opened door at Sergeant Evans. "Did you hear all this?" Evans touched his cap brim.

Then Upsher turned to Dot, "Miss Snareborn, I want you to think about something. Had you ever seen the substitute cab driver before? Would recognize him again?"

"Yes, I think I saw him twice before that night. He looks like a tradesman who came delivering cigars. Once, I saw him in the back garden. Clarissa was arguing with him, and their raised voices drew my attention. Later, I asked her who he was, and she said she bought my brother-in-law's cigars from him. I thought he was rather well dressed for someone who comes through the trade entrance." She stopped catching her breath and wiping her eyes before continuing.

"Another time, he stood on the street in front of the house talking to Gerald. I think he had been standing there for a while, so I noticed him. They walked down the street away from the house. Later, Gerald came to the door with an odd excuse about why he was late. We hadn't been getting along well because I had postponed our wedding until after my pinning as a graduate of the School of Nursing. So, I didn't argue with him. Thinking back, that was the first time I saw the man in the Homburg. It was the next day that he argued with Clarissa in the back garden."

Snow turned to Upsher. "I think that man is on Howard Street this morning. His name is Albert Sparks. Sparks is a gambler who loses. He owes money, may even owe Rolands who is good at cards. It is possible that Gerald Rolands and Clarissa Critchen hired him to murder Miss Snareborn before her birthday, allowing Clarissa to claim Dorothea's inheritance. Miss Snareborn had postponed her wedding to

Rolands once already. When she left to stay with Miss Cornman, they had to have known she would change her will and abandon her plans to marry. Either way, they would not come into the money that would make it possible for them to run away together."

Turning to Dot, he explained, "At that point, they may not have finalized their plan, but when you left, they had to make their move. If they asked after you at University Hospital, they likely discovered your plan to join Drs. Miles and Elliott. In their haste, they made mistakes. Sparks was not sure what you looked like. When Mary approached his cab, he thought she was you." Wide-eyed, both women nodded.

Snow continued, "Then he followed Mary down to St. Mary's County. He only found out she wasn't Dorothea after he abducted her, murdered her, and found the letter to Dr. Elliott which he burned. He may still be looking for you."

Upsher interrupted, "How do you know that Mary Flannery is dead?"

"I found her body in a run on my property. At the time, we didn't know who she was, but it was necessary to perform a burial. St. Mary's County Sheriff John Freeman has photographs of Mary Flannery taken at the time of her burial. A Pinkerton agent, Frank P. Geyer, sailed down to St. Mary's and consulted Sheriff Freeman concerning Miss Snareborn's disappearance. He has a copy of those photographs." Snow removed the photograph of nurses in the men's ward at University Hospital from Notes On Nursing and held it up to the women. "Is Mary Flannery in this photograph?"

Dot gasped and pointed to Mary Flannery. "The photograph is mine, the copy I gave to Mary. That's her standing just behind us. I gave her that book."

Snow turned to Commissioner Upsher. "A secretary in the office of the

Superintendent of Nurses at University Hospital also identified Mary Flannery in this photograph. I understand the Baltimore Police Department uses the Bertillon method of photography and measurement for identification. When I see Mr. Geyer this afternoon, we can obtain the copy of Sheriff Freeman's photographs."

Upsher raised his eyebrows. "So, Freeman uses photography and the Bertillon method? I'm impressed. I didn't think he even had a telegraph."

Snow smiled. "Sherriff John Freeman doesn't have a telegraph, but that's not his fault."

Upsher asked, "And the fiancé, Gerald Rolands, where is he?"

"He changed steamboats in the middle of the Bay and is in Fredericksburg, Virginia by now. At this point, I hope you are convinced that Dr. Elliott is not involved with the death of Mary Flannery."

Upsher's nodded, and Snow added, "Commissioner, are you armed?" Upsher undid his jacket buttons revealing a derringer. In the hallway, Evans drew his pistol.

"I have my police van waiting in the alley. We can take the ladies out through the back safely."

He called to Evans. "Sergeant, use the call box on the corner to tell the station house we are on our way. I want Dr. Elliott ready for identification when we arrive." At first, Evans hesitated but went out through the front door to comply.

Snow shifted in his chair but was reluctant to countermand the Commissioner of Baltimore Police.

Upsher added, "A patrolman and a driver are with the carriage. Sparks can hardly get by them."

Snow stood and thought, "They won't see what they are not looking for." But, he said, "I'll go first and scout the back yard.

Sparks may come down a service alley behind the house. I know what he looks like."

Snow led them out through the kitchen, unbuttoning his coat as he went. The others waited in the kitchen as he emerged onto the back porch. Hearing the patrolman and driver talking beside the house, he thought it unwise to approach them with his Police Pistol in hand. As he thought, a web of back alleys connected service entrances behind the houses where foot traffic could flow unseen from Madison Street. Delivery wagons, painters, carpenters, laundresses; all were coming and going unobserved from Howard Street as well.

Snow considered what Sparks knew. Sparks waited at Light Street when the *Northumberland* docked. He knew Rolands had not returned with the Pinkertons. He knew Dorothea Snareborn was still alive and Rolands or Clarissa wanted her dead.

Sparks would not attack her if she was escorted by Baltimore Police. At any rate, Snow last saw Sparks on Light Street. Evans returned, and Upsher escorted the two women down the steps behind Snow. At that moment, the butler came out of a basement entrance approaching the servant's privy. The women were both seated in the van when Snow became aware the butler was still staring into the opened outhouse door. Shock registered on the man's face as he turned toward Snow and stammered something unintelligible.

Snow pointed to the privy and waved the butler away from the opened door. "Commissioner, I think we may have found Sparks."

The butler stepped back and found his voice. "I think he's dead. We got a dead man in the privy!"

Evans and Upsher drew their weapons and approached. After a tense moment,

Upsher hailed Snow. "Judge Snow, can you identify this man for us?"

Snow approached and looked inside. A man soaked in his own blood lay collapsed against a wall. A pistol lay in his open hand. "I believe that is Sparks. At least, that is the man who waited on Light Street this morning. Miss Snareborn and Miss Cornman could make a better identification."

Upsher shook his head. "I don't need a couple of fainting women on my hands right now."

Snow explained. "They're nurses."

Upsher nodded. "Right. Miss Snareborn, Miss Cornman, would you please examine this man. I believe he is dead."

The two nurses not only identified Sparks, but also felt for a pulse, checked for respiration, unbuttoned the clothing and examined the wound. To Upsher's surprise, they admonished him to always check a patient's pulse and respiration before declaring an unconscious person deceased.

Dot Snareborn clarified their findings. "This man died in the last hour. The body is still warm, and most of the blood is still liquid. This happened while we were all talking in the parlor. He died when a long sharp blade plunged with force under his breast bone up into his heart. He may have died instantly as there is not the flow of blood normally found with stab wounds."

Snow thought, "Someone got very close to him before he drew that gun, someone he did not perceive as a threat, someone he did not recognize." He said, "Did he fire a shot? We didn't hear one."

Evans lifted the pistol from the dead man's hand using a pair of pliers from a tool box next to the privy. "It doesn't smell like it was fired. We would have heard a shot this close."

Upsher asked Evans, "What do you think he was stabbed with?"

Snow stared at the tool box and recalled the passenger who alighted from the streetcar with the cane. Quietly, almost to himself, Snow answered, "A cane." Leaning over the body, Evans and Upsher either didn't hear or didn't listen.

Snow escorted the nurses back to the van. Evans stayed with the corpse, and the patrolman called for a police wagon from the call box. Upsher, Snow, Miss Snareborn, and Miss Cornman drove a long silent ride to the Southern District Headquarters where Ben Elliott was held.

Upsher obtained Elliott's release that afternoon when Snow's influence expedited the hearing. The look on Elliott's face when he first laid eyes on Dot Snareborn was a reward in itself. Snow thought of Carrie, wished she was there to share the moment.

Later that evening, sipping Melrose alone in his back parlor, he realized Carrie had been in his thoughts all day, not Jane.

When Dot had thanked him, said she would forever be in his debt, he had asked her for the book. Now, Florence Nightingale's <u>Notes On Nursing</u> sat on his knee. He cut and lit his favorite IRABA and reminded himself. He had a promise to keep. He would bring it to her himself.

Snows Run

Afterwards the Recipes

Readers of Snow's Rest tell me they enjoy reading about how people lived in the early twentieth century. Especially they enjoy learning what people ate and how they cooked. Following my readers' guidance, I have enjoyed researching cookbooks and following recipes from the late 1800s and early 1900s. Included here are two favorite recipes of the ladies in Snow's Maryland Mysteries.

Jane Cawsin Snow's Puff Pastry Shells for Tarts

Puff Pastry

Wash hands first in very hot and then in very cold water. Measure four double handfuls and one single handful of white flour into a large sifter. Pinch in two measures of baking powder that fill the cupped well of one hand and the same amount of salt. Sift and then sift again. Fill one teacup full of butter and one teacup full of lard. Chill the tea cup of lard in a bowl of ice water until lard is hard. Soak hands in cold water. Rub cold lard into flour mixture until you have a fine paste. Add just enough ice water, say half a teacup, containing a beaten egg white. Mix until a stiff dough. Cut butter in four pieces. Sprinkle pastry board lightly with flour. Care should be taken to use as little flour as possible. More flour will make a tough curst. Roll paste thin and butter with one piece of butter. Sprinkle lightly with flour and roll it up like a scroll. Fold the ends into middle and roll out again. Repeat three more times until the butter is used up. Roll into a scroll again and place in an earthen bowl. Cover with a damp cloth and place in an icebox or springhouse an hour or more. It should be very cold before making out the crust. Tarts made will be flaky and difficult to cut.

Shells for Tarts

You will need two cookie cutters one large and one small. You may use a glass and a wine glass. The cutters should be dipped in hot water as you cut to make the edges rise when baked. Roll out puff pastry. Cut one large circle. Then cut three more and cut a hole in each with the smaller cutter. Lay these three on the first and bake at once.

Baking Shells

Heating of the oven is important. If you can hold your hand in the oven while counting to twenty, it is correctly heated. Another way to judge heat is to place a small piece of puff paste in oven and bake before baking the whole. The oven should stay heated while tarts are baking. Let bake ten or fifteen minutes until light brown.

Filling Tarts

Let cool and fill with preserves, jams, or marmalade. Filling now preserves the color and flavor of the filling.

Carrie Darberry's Cream Biscuits

In a four quart sifter place
2 double handfuls of white flour
Scatter enough sugar to fill a well in the middle
of your cupped hand over the flour
Repeat with baking powder

Linda A. Stewart

2 pinches of salt scattered over flour
Sift dry ingredients into a large bowl.

Fill tin mug with water about half your thumb
from bottom. Add 2 pinches of baking soda and
stir until it stops purring.

Skim 1 tin mug of cream from the top of last
night's slightly soured milk.   Add baking soda
water.

Make a well in the dry and slowly add the cream,
combining gently with a large spoon.
Lift dry into wet scraping the bottom until all the
flour is evenly wet.
Remember it isn't beating hard that makes the
biscuit nice. Beating hard kills the dough.
Pat the dough into a square half-inch cake on a
floured cutting board.
Cut in squares the size of the flat of your hand.
Place in separated rows on a baking sheet and
poke with a fork.
Bake in a quick oven.

Snows Run

About Linda Ann Stewart

Books, books, glorious books have always enriched my life. I grew up in an old country farm house with a fireplace in every room, no closets, and many bookshelves. I read with a flashlight under the covers late into the night, well past my bedtime. At the end of a summer morning caring for the family's gentle dairy cows, my greatest reward was a walk to the town library. After graduating from Bridgewater State College, I spent forty years sharing my love of books with children, those I taught and those I raised. So, I thought, "Now is the time!" Retiring to experience books from the other side of the cover, I was delighted with the reception given my first novel, <u>Snow's Rest, A Maryland Mystery</u>. Now, the second novel in the series, <u>Snow's Run, A Maryland Mystery</u> is ready to greet my readers. Readers will find William Snow and Carrie Darberry moving on with their lives along the ebb and flow of St. Mary's River and into another mystery.